"I Wish You

"Once I start, Sunday, I won't want to stop,"
Simon warned her.

"Neither will I."

"If I kiss you, I'll want to touch you."

"I'll want to touch you, too."

"If I touch you, I can damn well guarantee I'm
going to want to make love to you."

"That makes two of us."

Before Sunday could think about what she was
saying, Simon kissed her. All her surroundings
receded until there was just Simon, with his
smooth, cajoling, intoxicating mouth. Simon with
his strong, nimble, caressing fingers. Simon with
hands that knew exactly where to touch her—and
how. Simon with his hard, muscular, incredibly
masculine body.

"Are we crazy?" she whispered against his lips.

"Yes…"

Dear Reader:

Welcome to Silhouette Desire - provocative, compelling, contemporary love stories written by and for today's woman. These are stories to treasure.

Each and every Silhouette Desire is a wonderful romance in which the emotional and the sensual go hand in hand. When you open a Desire, you enter a whole new world - a world that has, naturally, a perfect hero just waiting to whisk you away! A Silhouette Desire can be light-hearted or serious, but it will always be satisfying.

We hope you enjoy this Desire today - and will go on to enjoy many more.

Please write to us:

Jane Nicholls
Silhouette Books
PO Box 236
Thornton Road
Croydon
Surrey
CR9 3RU

The Maddening Model

SUZANNE SIMMS

*First published in Great Britain in 1995
by Silhouette Books, Eton House, 18-24 Paradise Road,
Richmond, Surrey TW9 1SR*

© Suzanne Simmons Guntrum 1995

*Silhouette, Silhouette Desire and Colophon are
Trade Marks of Harlequin Enterprises II B.V.*

ISBN 0 373 05923 X

22-9509

Made and printed in Great Britain

SUZANNE SIMMS

is the award-winning author of more than thirty romance novels. She has travelled extensively, including a memorable trip to the Philippines, which, she says, "changed my life." Suzanne currently lives with her husband, her son and her cat, Merlin, in Indiana. She also writes historical romances as Suzanne Simmons.

Other Silhouette Books by Suzanne Simms

Silhouette Desire

Moment in Time
Of Passion Born
A Wild, Sweet Magic
All Night Long
So Sweet a Madness
Only this Night
Dream Within a Dream
Nothing Ventured
Moment of Truth
Not *His* Wedding!
Not *Her* Wedding!
*The Brainy Beauty
*The Pirate Princess

Hazards, Inc.

This one is for Jayne Ann Krentz,
whose friendship through the years
has been worth more to me than
diamonds or emeralds, rubies or sapphires.

One

She stuck out like a sore thumb...from the tips of her three-hundred-dollar handmade Italian leather sandals to the top of her very red head.

The essence of casual chic, she was dressed in pink silk trousers and a pink silk shirt. A designer handbag was tossed over one shoulder—he couldn't quite make out the initials embossed on the front—and a pair of designer sunglasses were perched on the end of her nose.

Her sunglasses probably cost more *baht* than the average Thai worker made in a year, Simon Hazard judged as he leaned back in the rickety chair, balancing his weight on its rear legs.

Legs.

Hers were long and lean and lithe. He could tell that much from the way she walked.

Every eye in the Celestial Palace was on her. Little wonder. It wasn't every day that a six-foot-tall amazon with hair the color of a blazing sunset sauntered into the back-street Bangkok bar.

What in the bloody hell was a woman like that *doing in a place like* this?

Simon shook his head, picked up the glass of beer in front of him and took a drink. It was none of his business. *She* was none of his business. He was here to meet a client. Nothing more. Nothing less.

Pushing his cap back off his face—the USN printed across the front identified it as one left over from the days when he'd served in the United States navy for Uncle Sam aboard a nuclear-powered sub—he took another swig of his beer. It was a local brew—strong, pungent, dark in color and served at room temperature. Unfortunately, it was the hot season in this part of the world and the crowded bar was like a steam bath.

An ice-cold beer on a sweltering hot day was one of the things he genuinely missed about the States, Simon reflected as he looked around the pub.

A trio of noisy sailors had bellied up to the bar and were egging one another on as they downed straight shots of Russian vodka. There were two suspicious-looking characters hunched over a nearby table, arguing in a language he didn't recognize. It wasn't Thai or Chinese or Malay, and it certainly wasn't English, the four principal languages spoken in this country once known as Siam. Bar girls of every size and shape, most of them dressed in cheap, skintight dresses and teetering on three-inch high heels, were serving watered-down drinks to the customers. An ancient jukebox in the corner was blaring the same tune over and over again. It was a young Elvis Presley singing about a "fool such as I."

Simon stared bemusedly into his beer. Maybe, just maybe, the "King of Rock 'n' Roll" was alive and well and living somewhere in the Upper Peninsula of Michigan the way the tabloids claimed.

Or maybe Simon was losing the last remnants of his sanity.

He must be. Here he was, sitting in a seedy bar in the red-light district of a city known for its sex and sin, a compact revolver on the inside of his belt and a small but very sharp stiletto tucked into his right boot, waiting for some damned fool who'd gotten it into his head that he wanted to see the high mountain country between Thailand and what was once called Burma and was now known as Myanmar.

Answer a fool according to his folly.

Simon took another swallow of tepid alcohol. Which one of them was the greater fool? His client, the mysterious Mr. S. Harrington, or himself?

"As long as you're playing Twenty Questions, what the hell are you doing half a world away from home, you crazy son of a bitch?" Simon muttered under his breath.

But he knew the answer to his own question. He was on the job. For a nominal fee, he would drive his beat-up Range Rover and its passengers anywhere and everywhere they wanted to go.

Although he hadn't always been a glorified guide/ hired driver in a third world country, of course.

One morning, over a year ago, Simon Hazard had awakened in his penthouse apartment overlooking Minneapolis on one side and the mighty Mississippi River on the other, and realized that he was burned-out on his business, on what passed for pleasure in his life and on life itself. It had not, as he recalled, made for a great thirty-first birthday.

So he had packed his bags and gone off to "get in touch with his feelings," as the pop psychologists labeled it.

He'd spent one entire year wandering among the saffron-robed Buddhist monks, the ancient temples and the golden spires of the Lotus Kingdom: Thailand. He'd made friends with the hill tribes of the North, lived in a primitive hut with a thatched roof, eaten food cooked over a fire fueled by dried water-buffalo dung and learned to use a machete like an expert.

He now spoke the language, knew the customs, was beginning to understand the people. He could defend himself against the Siamese crocodile and the armed bandits who sometimes roamed the Golden Triangle. He knew when the king cobra was in season and how to avoid the fifteen-foot-long, lightning fast serpent with its fatal bite. He understood it was a gross insult to point his toe at someone, according to Thai thinking, and that the national pastime was gambling, whether it was on a cockfight or a boxing match.

As a boy, he had once searched out the source of the Mississippi: Lake Itasca. As a man, he had gone in search of something more elusive. What he had discovered was a simpler time and place, and a people who hadn't changed in hundreds of years.

What he had found, Simon reflected, was himself.

"Must be the alcohol making me wax philosophical," he said by way of an explanation, gazing down into the dregs of his drink.

There was an insistent tug on his sleeve. "Hey, boss, you want another beer?"

Simon turned his head. A boy of eight or nine was standing beside him.

He didn't want another drink, but there was something about the kid, something about his eyes.

"Sure." Simon flipped him a coin. "And keep the change."

The small face broke into a huge grin. "Thanks, boss. Beer right away."

Maybe the hardest lesson he'd had to learn in the past year was that he couldn't rescue everyone like this street kid. So he did what he could.

"Which isn't very much, is it, Hazard?" he acknowledged as the boy set the glass down, brown liquor sloshing over the sides, and took off with his newfound wealth.

He couldn't do anything about the boy, but he could—and *would*—do something about the woman.

Simon watched as the redhead approached the man behind the bar. Damn, if there wasn't something familiar about her. He had the strongest sensation that he'd seen her before.

He stared unabashedly. Why not? Everybody else in the Celestial Palace was. Not that it seemed to bother

her. She appeared oblivious to the stares and the whispers. This was a woman, he realized, who was used to being noticed, who *expected* to be noticed.

She slid her sunglasses up into her hair and looked directly at the bartender. The noise level dropped off for an instant and Simon clearly heard her say, in a voice that sent cool shivers down his spine, "Perhaps you can help me. I'm looking for someone."

The man answered in accented English, "Looking for who, lady?"

The din of voices, clinking glasses and a crooning Elvis Presley picked up again. She leaned over the counter and said something Simon couldn't make out.

The bartender raised his hand and pointed. He was pointing in the direction of Simon's table.

She turned. Without the sun at her back, without the dark glasses obscuring her features, Simon saw her clearly for the first time. She was stunning, but not in any conventional sense of the word. Her hair was too red. Her eyes were too green. Her cheekbones were too prominent. Her nose was too aristocratic. Her mouth was almost too perfect.

He had seen that face before.

His gaze dropped to her slender shoulders, her generous breasts, her slim waist, her long, long legs.

He had seen that body before. He could swear it.

She walked toward him, stopped in front of his table and looked down her nose at him. "Are you Simon Hazard?"

He refused to alter his expression. "What if I am?"

"I believe we have an appointment, Mr. Hazard."

"An appointment?"

"For three o'clock."

He resisted the urge to glance at his watch. "Is it three o'clock already?"

"Five minutes past," she said, consulting the slim gold band on her wrist.

"Time flies when you're having fun," he muttered dryly.

"Are you?"

"Am I what?" He snorted and drained his glass to the last drop. "Having fun?"

Apparently, she chose to ignore his attempt at making a witticism. "Are you Simon Hazard?"

He might as well confess. "The one and only."

She thrust out her right hand. Simon wondered if he was supposed to shake it or kiss it. "I'm Sunday Harrington," she informed him.

Sunday. He supposed, with a name like that, she'd heard them all.

Sunday, fun day.

Sunday in the park with George.

Solomon Grundy buried on Sunday.

Sunday afternoon.

Sunday school.

Sunday's child.

Never on Sunday.

"Sunday Harrington?" The name rang a bell. He studied the initials on her handbag: a stylized, intertwining S and H. Then it suddenly dawned on him. "S. Harrington stands for Sunday Harrington."

"Brilliant deduction."

He bit off a brief and rather crude expletive. The legs of his chair hit the floor of the Celestial Palace with a resounding thud. "I assumed the S stood for Sidney or Sheldon or Stanley."

"You assumed incorrectly."

His eyes narrowed. "You're not a man."

She seemed to be biting the corners of her mouth. "I'm not a man. I would think that was obvious, even to you."

It was.

"You're my client."

"I'm your client."

Bloody hell, she was his client.

That's when he recalled reading in the newspapers—it had been a few years ago now—about a fashion model who always dressed in pink or purple or red, despite conventional wisdom that redheads should avoid those colors.

That's when Simon Hazard remembered the last time he'd seen this woman. She had been larger than life, literally, and she had been wearing several tiny scraps of purple material that left little, if anything, to the imagination.

Simon blew out his breath expressively. As a matter of fact, the first *and* last time he had seen Sunday Harrington, she had been wearing next to nothing....

Two

She'd made a mistake.

A big mistake.

A *huge* mistake.

"There must be some mistake," she said, swallowing hard.

A small, mocking smile appeared on the man's lips. "You can say that again."

"But you're a—" She was too polite, Sunday reminded herself, to say he was a two-bit cowboy, an unshaven slob, a disreputable character and very possibly a drunkard, besides. She took a deep breath. "But you're an American."

He flashed her *that* smile again. "Born and raised in the heartland of the U.S.A.—Minneapolis, Minnesota."

"You're not Thai."

"I would think that was obvious, even to you," he said, his voice laced with sarcasm.

Sunday stood a little straighter, not that she had ever been one to slouch. "I assumed you would be Thai."

"You assumed incorrectly."

The situation was getting awkward. "I thought my secretary made my requirements clear. I want someone who speaks the language, understands the customs and knows his way around this country." The man just sat there. "What I want, Mr. Hazard," she said, no longer mincing words, "is the best."

There was a flash of straight, white teeth. "Lady, that's what you've got—the best."

What she had, Sunday realized, was a problem. And a *big* problem, at that. From where she stood—and he sat—it was apparent that Simon Hazard was tall, well over six feet tall, broad-shouldered, long-legged and handsome as sin . . . if a woman was partial to the rugged he-man type, which, thankfully, she was not.

He stuck out like a sore thumb from the tips of his scuffed cowboy boots to the top of his head. His hair was blue-black and long at the nape; it was damp from the heat and formed dark curls that brushed against the collar of his denim shirt every time he moved his head. She wondered when he had last had a haircut.

There was at least a two day's growth of beard on his chin. His jaw was chiseled granite and decidedly uncompromising. His nose—possibly his best feature—was a throwback to some patrician ancestor. His eyes were dark, somewhere between brown and black.

They were bright, intelligent and unclouded by the alcohol he had consumed.

Unfortunately, his clothes looked as if he'd slept in them, and there was no doubt he had an attitude. His body, his face, his expression, his eyes all spelled one thing: danger.

Sunday's heart sank.

"I don't think this is going to work, Mr. Hazard." She permitted herself a small sigh. "You can simply return my deposit and we'll go our separate ways."

"Can't."

"Can't or won't?"

"Can't."

"Why not?"

"Drank it." He indicated the glass of brown liquor on the table in front of him. "Beer."

"You *drank* the entire deposit?" She was shocked, and she made no attempt to hide it. "But I sent several hundred *baht* with the messenger only this morning."

His eyes narrowed. "It seems you haven't done your arithmetic, Ms. Harrington. A hundred-*baht* note is the equivalent of only four American dollars."

Sunday didn't know what to say. "Oh—"

"And, in case you also didn't notice, the prices around here are inflated for a *farang*."

She still didn't know what to say to him. She finally managed to inquire, "A *farang?*"

"A stranger." Simon Hazard leaned back in his chair again and balanced his weight on the spindly rear legs. "Besides, you won't find anyone better."

"That is a matter of opinion."

"*That* is a matter of fact." He stroked his jawline. "Tell me something."

She waited for him to go on.

"Why would a woman like you want to travel into the hinterlands of Thailand, anyway?"

"Business," she said.

"Business? What kind of business?" Suspicion was thick in his voice. "It better not have anything to do with the poppy."

Sunday drew a blank. "The poppy?"

"Opium."

Her mouth dropped open, whether in surprise or outrage, she wasn't sure. "You think I'm involved with drugs?"

"I don't know what to think, do I?" He gave her a stony stare. "I don't know anything about you."

"I assure you, Mr. Hazard, my business is strictly legitimate," she retorted, bristling.

He shrugged but said nothing.

Her temper flared. "Keep the damned deposit, then. I'll find someone else."

"No."

"No?"

"We've got a deal, Ms. Harrington. Signed, sealed and delivered. You pay. I guide."

He was right. She had received an agreement through the mail and she'd signed it.

Sunday permitted herself another small sigh. If she wanted to do business, if she wanted to see the crafts produced by the hill tribes, if she wanted to visit the City of Mist, if she wanted to experience the closest thing to heaven on earth, it was, apparently, going to be in the company of this cowboy.

"All right, we still have a deal, Mr. Hazard," she said, holding out her hand.

He moved surprisingly fast for a big man. His chair was upright and he was on his feet, pumping her arm, before she knew it. "Business is business," he said.

Sunday looked around the bar. "Is this where you usually conduct your business dealings?"

"There's nothing wrong with the Celestial Palace," he countered in a hard, dry voice.

As if on cue, a fight broke out between two sailors at the bar. There was the sound of breaking glass and voices raised in anger. The bartender shouted, "Stop! Stop!" and pounded the bar with his fist, but no one paid him any heed. Somewhere, a girl let out a shriek.

"The Celestial Palace isn't exactly a slice of heaven," Sunday observed judiciously.

"Let's get out of here," he said.

"Where are we going?" she inquired as he took her by the elbow and steered her toward the door.

"Does it matter?"

"Of course, it matters."

"We're going someplace where we're less conspicuous. Someplace where we can talk and not have half the people in the room eavesdropping on our conversation. You never know who might be in a watering hole like this. Thieves. Smugglers. Pickpockets."

With long-legged strides, Simon Hazard took off down the street. Sunday was nearly running to keep up with him. "I thought you said there was nothing wrong with the Celestial Palace."

He threw her a sharp glance. "'Before you trust a man, eat a peck of salt with him.'"

"I beg your pardon."

"'The road up and the road down is one and the same,'" he stated cryptically.

Sunday's handbag—one of her own popular designs—slipped off her shoulder. She pushed the leather strap up her arm and kept going. "What does the road have to do with anything?"

"'Answer a fool according to his folly.'"

"I'd settle for a simple, straightforward answer," she muttered under her breath.

"'It is not every question that deserves an answer.'"

"Tell me, wherever did you—"

"Monks."

"Monks?"

"I spent my first year in Thailand—in Prathet Thai—with Buddhist monks," he told her as if that would explain everything.

It explained nothing.

He hailed a passing *samlor,* a three-wheel taxi that was a common sight in Bangkok, and gave instructions to the driver in Thai. Then, off they went through a labyrinth of narrow streets, dodging people, animals and other vehicles alike.

Simon Hazard leaned toward her and remarked conversationally, "Bangkok—Krung Thep—is a paradox."

Bangkok wasn't the only paradox, Sunday thought.

He went on. "It is both ancient and modern, Eastern and Western, sacred and profane. Skyscrapers have grown up alongside buildings of traditional Thai architecture. Contemporary shops of every type and description are next to the famous Floating Market, its boats bobbing on the *khlongs,* or canals, as they have for centuries.'' He pulled the bill of his hat down to shade his eyes from the tropical sun. ''Bangkok is a city of six million souls. It is a city teeming with myriad sights, sounds and smells.''

''*Krung Thep* means 'City of Angels,' doesn't it?'' she said, recalling what she'd read in her *Fodor's Guide to Thailand.*

''That's the shortened version. Bangkok has the longest place name in the world. The literal translation is 'Great City of Angels, Supreme Repository of Divine Jewels, the Great and Unconquerable Land, Grand and Illustrious Realm, Royal and Delightful Capital City...''' His voice trailed off. ''There's more, but I think you get the idea.''

''Yes, I think I do,'' she said, sitting back in the taxi. ''How long have you been in Thailand, Mr. Hazard?''

''Simon. A little over a year. And you?''

''Three days.'' She took a silk fan from her handbag, opened it and wafted it back and forth in front of her face. ''I confess, most of that time has been spent in my hotel room recovering from jet lag and trying to adjust to the heat.''

''This is the hot season.'' Something flickered behind the man's eyes. ''The good news is it's cooler up in the hills where we're going.''

''What's the bad news?''

"The central plain of Thailand lies within the 'rain shadow' of the Burmese mountains."

"Meaning—"

"It's wet."

Sunday tried not to wrinkle up her nose. "Wet?"

"It rains a lot."

"I'm not made of spun sugar, Mr. Hazard. I won't melt."

"Simon," he reminded her.

"Simon."

He seemed to be choosing his words with care. "Then there's the king cobra."

Sunday cast him a sidelong glance. "What about the king cobra?"

"It can grow to be eighteen feet long—" Simon spread his arms wide "—and weigh twenty pounds."

She shrugged. "In other words, it's a big snake."

"The largest of all venomous snakes. Fortunately, the king cobra doesn't like to be around people."

"Lucky for us."

"As a matter of fact, very few cobra bites are reported," he assured her.

"More good news," she said happily.

Simon's expression was deadpan. "Probably because none of the victims survived for more than an hour unless they were treated with antivenin."

Sunday wasn't about to be frightened off. "I promise I'll be very careful where I step."

There was a short pause. "I feel it's also only fair to warn you about the elephants."

"They're big, too, aren't they?"

Simon didn't appear to be amused. "If four tons of enraged animal—ears flapping, trunk raised, tusks aimed at your breast—charges at an unexpected sprint, you won't be making jokes, Ms. Harrington."

"Sunday."

"Sunday." His mouth curved humorlessly. "You haven't seen rage until you've seen an elephant in *musth.*"

She had to ask. "What is *musth?*"

"It's a state of sexual arousal in male elephants that can last for days, sometimes weeks or even months. The bull's testosterone level may increase sixtyfold."

Sunday was nonplussed.

Simon continued. "The first rule of the forest is never take an elephant for granted."

It seemed like a reasonable rule to her.

"Then there's the dung," he added.

"Dung?"

"Elephant manure."

She made an impatient noise. "I know what dung is."

He arched one dark eyebrow. "An elephant defecates as often as twenty-eight times a day."

She hadn't known, of course. It wasn't the kind of information considered useful in the fashion world. "It must make for a great deal of dung."

"Unflappable," Simon announced.

"What is?"

"You are."

She stopped fanning herself for a moment and knitted her eyebrows. "Was this some kind of test?"

"You might call it that."

"I take it I passed."

"With flying colors. Like I said, you're unflappable."

"Not unflappable. Determined." She folded her lips in a soft, obstinate line. "It's the only way I know how to be. It's got me where I am today."

"Which is where?"

"Successful beyond my wildest dreams."

He stared at her intently. "What brought you to Thailand, Sunday Harrington?"

She told him the truth. "I want to see the City of Mist." She met and held his gaze. "What brought you to Thailand a year ago, Simon Hazard?"

"I was looking for something."

So was she.

"Have you found it?" she inquired.

"Yes." The *samlor* came to a halt. "We're here," he informed her.

"Where?" she asked as she took his proffered hand and stepped out of the taxi.

"Wat Po."

Three

"The Temple of the Reclining Buddha," Simon translated as they entered the grounds near the Grand Palace with its complex of exotic buildings, dozens of pagodas and distinctive gilded spires.

Sunday stopped, put her head back and stared up at the colossal golden Buddha resting on its side. "Why, it's . . . it's . . . huge!"

"One hundred and fifty feet long, and fifty feet high," Simon informed her.

Sunday had never seen anything like it before. "It's magnificent!" she exclaimed.

He agreed. "Yes, it is. There are nearly four hundred Buddhist temples in the city of Bangkok, and countless statues of the Buddha. The Emerald Buddha is the most revered. The Golden Buddha is the most valuable—it's solid gold and weighs more than ten thousand pounds. But the Reclining Buddha is the most unusual.''

Sunday was no expert, but she'd done her reading before traveling to Thailand. ''I thought the Buddha was always depicted in a meditative sitting position.''

''Usually, but not always. That's the primary reason the Reclining Buddha is considered unique.'' Simon reached for a stick of incense and lit the end in a brazier at the base of the statue. A thin trail of scented smoke spiraled up from the altar toward the ceiling. ''The statue is gold leaf over plaster. The feet are inlaid with gemstones representing the one hundred and eight attributes of the Buddha. And why the reclining position? It's the final stage of the Buddha's passage to nirvana.''

''To heaven,'' Sunday murmured.

''To heaven,'' he echoed.

They stood in silence for several minutes, and then left the temple to stroll among the guardians—huge stone warriors standing at attention before the royal buildings—the saffron-robed Buddhist monks, those who had come to offer their prayers and homage, the merely curious and the tourists.

Sunday glanced at Simon out of the corner of her eye. ''Why did you bring me here?''

''I told you. I wanted to take you someplace where we were less conspicuous.''

She snorted softly. ''There isn't anyplace where a man like you and a woman like me are going to be inconspicuous.''

''You have a point,'' he conceded.

"I had to face facts a long time ago," she admitted to him. "I wasn't going to be cute."

"Did you want to be cute?"

"Yes. For a week or two, anyway." She laughed at the short-lived girlhood dream. "But I quickly realized I was never going to be cute or dainty, petite or fragile. I was never going to pass unnoticed in a crowd. I was always going to stick out like a sore thumb."

She knew Simon was watching; she could feel his eyes on her. "How old were you when you reached this conclusion?" he asked.

"Thirteen."

He grimaced. "An awkward age."

"Especially awkward for a girl who stood a head taller than anyone else in her class at school," she related with an emotional detachment that had come with experience and maturity.

"So—" he shrugged "—you were tall."

"It was more than that," she confessed. "I had the neck of a giraffe. My shoe size was a ten, extra narrow. And I was covered from head to toe with freckles."

"You may have been an ugly duckling, but you turned into a swan in the end," he said appreciatively.

She deftly changed the subject. "When did you realize you were different?"

"Am I?"

She laughed out loud again. "Of course, adolescent boys want to tower over everyone else, don't they?"

"I didn't."

"You didn't what?"

"I didn't realize I was different."

"Why not?"

"My family."

"Explain."

"All the Hazard men—that adds up to nearly a dozen if we count uncles, cousins, nephews and brothers—are tall."

They both knew there was more to it than height. It was height *and* a commanding presence.

She was genuinely curious. "Don't you have any women in your family?"

Simon frowned. "Only those we've convinced to marry into the clan." He went on. "My nephew, Jonathan, married a brilliant Egyptologist just before I left the States."

Surely any nephew of this man's would still be a boy. "Your nephew would be how old?"

He thought for half a minute. "Thirty-seven. Maybe thirty-eight by now."

Sunday was baffled. "How...?"

"It's one of those generational-gap things," he said inconclusively.

She arched one eyebrow. "What is a generational-gap thing?"

Simon lifted his massive shoulders, and then dropped them again. "My father married five times and had five sons. Avery is the oldest. I'm the youngest. There's a thirty-year gap between us. Avery's two sons, Jonathan and Nick, are both older than I am."

"I see."

They walked past another group of delicately carved pagodas, a traditional Thai garden with immaculately trimmed trees and shrubs, huge stone urns of colorful flowers and life-size statues of elephants and water buffalo.

"As a matter of fact, it's thanks to Jonathan that I'm in Thailand," he said at last.

"Did he vacation here, and then entice you with tales of his travels?"

"Not exactly."

She waited, assuming he would tell her more.

He did.

"I don't know the whole story," Simon began. "I don't think anyone does, with the exception of Jonathan, and he's real closemouthed about it. All I heard is that his old nemesis finally caught up with him in a back alley here in Bangkok several years ago. Jonathan was fished out of the *khlongs* the next morning by a friendly local, and spent a month in the hospital recuperating from his dip in the canals."

Sunday was stunned. "Someone beat him up?"

"Somebody beat him to a bloody pulp." Simon paused and stared off into the distance. There was something implacable about the way he stood there, something unnerving in his eyes and in the square set of his jaw. She wouldn't want to be this man's enemy. She wouldn't want to be Jonathan Hazard's old nemesis, if Simon ever caught up with him. "Not literally to a bloody pulp," he said finally. "There wasn't a visible scratch on him. All his injuries were internal."

She tried to swallow and found it impossible. "He must have been badly hurt."

"He was half-dead." Simon shook his head from side to side. "Make that closer to three-quarters."

"Is Jonathan all right now?"

"Good as gold. Right as rain. Has been for ages."

She was relieved.

"Anyway, what impressed him about Thailand was the warmth and hospitality of its people. He wasn't used to that in his line of work."

Sunday's hand fluttered to her breast. "Is Jonathan—" she lowered her voice to a whisper "—a spy?"

"Was." Simon walked on. "At least, that's the rumor."

"He's your nephew and you don't know for certain."

"I never asked. He never said."

"Men!"

"What's that supposed to mean?"

Even if she tried to explain it, he would never understand. Sunday threw up her hands. "Men!"

Simon wasn't sure when he first became aware that they were being followed. It had started with a slight niggling sensation at the back of his neck, a mere pinprick of awareness.

Instinct.

The men in his family had an instinct for trouble. It was a kind of sixth sense, an inexplicable talent for spotting a disaster before it happened. Maybe it was the reason so many of them had made danger their business.

By the time they'd left the Temple of the Reclining Buddha, Simon was certain.

Three paces behind them.

Small wiry man.

Thai.

Dressed in dark trousers, white shirt, brown sandals.

Black hair. Black eyes. Nondescript features. Nevertheless, Simon had seen him somewhere before.

The Celestial Palace.

"Damn!" he swore, making a production of removing his hat, taking a linen handkerchief from his back pocket and mopping the perspiration from his forehead.

"It's hot, isn't it?" Sunday remarked, retrieving a tissue from her handbag and blotting her upper lip.

"Yes. Let's grab some shade," he suggested, reaching for her hand and urging her toward a stone bench beneath a copse of trees. He wanted to see what the man shadowing them would do next.

"I thought I knew everything there was to know about what heat and humidity can do to a woman's disposition, but I was wrong," Sunday said, taking a silk fan from her handbag.

She waved the fan back and forth in front of her. It created a slight breeze that carried her scent to his nostrils.

Simon breathed in deeply. Sunday Harrington smelled of exotic incense, tropical heat, warm silk and . . . roses, of all things. It took a great deal of self-control—more than he thought he had, for a minute—not to bend over and nuzzle her neck, or to bury his face in the inviting cleavage between her breasts.

Son-of-a-gun! Maybe he'd been gone from home too long. Maybe his vow of celibacy, however temporary or sensible under the circumstances—he was living like a Buddhist Monk—was backfiring after more than a year. One thing was certain: he'd better get a grip on himself.

"I promise it will be cooler up in the mountains," Simon said, clearing his throat.

"I hope so."

He was aware that she sat there quietly, calmly, observing everything around her. She had the ability to sit utterly still, to simply *be*. It wasn't a trait he often saw in Westerners.

He was also aware of their shadow. The man had paused some twenty feet away and was making a pretense of studying the rock garden.

"It's very peaceful here," Sunday finally said.

"Beneath the noise, the pollution, the traffic of Bangkok, there is a sense of serenity. Most people believe it's the calming influence of Buddhism." Simon removed his cap again and ran his fingers through his hair. "However, appearances can sometimes be deceiving."

"Everything isn't always what it seems to be."

"*Or* everyone," he suggested.

"You mean like the man who's been tailing us since we left the Celestial Palace?"

He was taken aback. "How did you know?"

"For our own safety, we women have had to develop a sixth sense about that kind of thing," she said.

"I must say, he looks harmless enough. I wonder what he wants."

"Probably your handbag."

"I can't imagine why. It doesn't match his outfit," she teased, flashing him a smile.

"Here he comes. I'll do the talking. You keep an eye on your purse," Simon warned.

"I hardly think a purse snatcher would try to strike up a conversation first," she said.

The man halted several feet from them. He bowed politely and said to Simon in excellent English, "If you were guests in my humble home, I would offer a glass of water to you and to your lady."

"A glass of water would be greatly appreciated," Simon responded with the same excruciating politeness.

The newcomer's expression was enigmatic. "'The man who possesses a good wife, possesses a good thing.'"

Simon looked at him with steady eyes. "The lady is not my wife."

He tried again. "'The man who has good health is young.'"

Sunday leaned toward him and murmured in his ear, "Are you healthy?"

Talking out of the side of his mouth, he said to her, "As a horse." He turned his full attention back to their shadow.

"'A coward turns away, but a brave man's choice is danger,'" the man said this time.

"'A living dog is better than a dead tiger,'" Simon responded with the same degree of inscrutability.

"'The day is for honest men, the night for thieves.'"

Beside him, Sunday made an impatient sound. "Don't tell me this man spent a year living with the monks, as well."

The Thai gentleman turned to her and responded, "Indeed, I did, gracious lady. It is our custom."

"Almost all Thai males spend at least part of their adolescence in a Buddhist monastery, taking vows of celibacy and poverty," Simon explained. "Some decide it is their karma. They end up becoming monks. The rest return to the outside world."

"Do you all learn to speak in proverbs?"

Simon ignored her.

But the stranger answered, "Truth is truth." Then he lifted his hands beseechingly, with the palms up, and continued pleading his case. "You must understand, sir, that I have a wife and five children to feed and clothe."

Simon put his hands together and interlaced his fingers. "You have many responsibilities."

"A great many responsibilities. So many that I cannot leave my family and journey to the north."

"It is a long journey, and the road leading up the mountains is difficult."

"Just a little while ago, you said the road up and the road down are one and the same," interjected Sunday.

Simon didn't look at her, but he said through clenched teeth, "It has also been said that there are two days when a woman is a pleasure—the day one marries her and the day one buries her."

That had the desired effect. It shut Sunday up.

"I regret that my station in life—I am but a lowly clerk—prevents me from giving it to you as a gift," the man stated.

Simon was very careful not to react.

The Thai gentleman went on. "It is said that you were a stranger among us. Yet you learned to speak our language and understand our ways. You are no longer a *farang*."

"Thank you."

"You are a businessman."

"I am a businessman."

"Then you will not miss the few insubstantial *baht* that I must regrettably ask in exchange. It is worth a fortune to one who is enterprising."

He was enterprising, all right.

"Only a few men see the world that can be theirs for the asking. You are one of these men, are you not, sir?"

Simon inclined his head slightly. Flattery: a very old and useful tool in negotiations.

The man stepped into the shade of a tree, dived into his pocket and brought out a small silk pouch. He carefully opened the top and withdrew a piece of paper which appeared to be old and yellowed.

Simon was curious, in spite of himself. "What is it?"

"It is a riddle. It is a map."

"Where will this map lead me?"

"It will lead you to happiness and riches."

Simon didn't move a muscle. "Could you be more specific?"

"It will take you to the Hidden Buddha of the Heavenly Mist," the map seller claimed.

Simon allowed his skepticism to show. "I have not heard of this hidden Buddha."

An inscrutable smile surfaced on the man's ageless features. "Then it is well named, is it not?"

Simon was far from convinced. "Possibly."

Reassurance was immediately forthcoming. "All that I have said is true."

Simon rubbed his hand back and forth along his chin. "I will give you one hundred *baht* for the piece of paper."

The man appeared stunned. "But it is worth many times that, and I have a wife and six children to feed and clothe."

"I thought you said you had five children."

The man became animated. "There is my sister's son who came to visit my home a year ago and now will not leave. I did not count him before."

"Two hundred *baht*."

"My eldest daughter is of marriageable age. I must be able to afford the temple offerings and the wedding feast."

"Three hundred."

Sunday opened her handbag and dug around for a moment. Simon assumed she was searching for another tissue. Instead, she brought out a fistful of money and said to the man, "I will give you one thousand *baht* for the map."

His eyes darted from Simon to Sunday and back again. "But..."

Simon heaved a sigh of defeat and indicated his consent. "One thousand *baht* it is, then."

The small man handed over the map and accepted his money in exchange. He bowed several times and intoned, "May enlightenment be yours, most generous lady, and yours, sir."

Then he turned and quickly disappeared into the crowd.

"You paid too much," Simon told her.

"That is a matter of opinion."

"The paper is worthless."

"Very probably."

He knew she was no fool. "Then why give the man a thousand *baht* for it?"

"For the same reason you were going to give him three hundred," Sunday answered.

He sat and he waited.

She went on to explain. "Maybe the man really does have a wife and five children to feed and clothe."

Simon crossed his arms and stretched his legs out in front of him. "Six. Don't forget his sister's son."

Sunday lifted the weight of her hair off her neck in a graceful motion that caught—and held—his attention. "Let's look at what we got for one thousand *baht,* shall we?"

He grunted. "Why not?"

The scrap of paper was carefully unfolded and smoothed out flat on her lap. "It's appears to be a map." She pointed to the bottom of the page. "And these are some kind of symbols."

"The man said it was a map *and* a riddle." Simon studied the crude drawing first. "I believe I recognize this area." He indicated a serpentine line down the middle.

Sunday's red eyebrows, the same color as her hair, drew together. "What is it?"

"The river Pai."

She raised her eyes to his; they really were the most incredible shade of green he'd ever seen. "And where is the river Pai?" she asked.

He concentrated on his answer. "In the north."

"Anywhere near where we're headed?"

"Yes."

"How near?"

He wouldn't lie to her. He wasn't sure he could. "Very near. Not far from Mae Hong Son."

She wrinkled up her forehead again. "Mae Hong Son?"

"The City of Mist."

She gnawed on her lower lip. "That is amazing."

"Amazing," he repeated, unable to keep the sardonic tone from his voice.

Her chin came up. A faint color rose in her cheeks. Perhaps her skin had once been covered with freckles, but it was like peaches and cream now. "You sound a little . . . skeptical."

He was more than a little skeptical; he was a lot skeptical. "That's because I am."

"Why?"

"It's too much of a coincidence."

"What is?"

Simon raised his eyes upward in a silent plea for patience. "We're headed for the City of Mist. A stranger appears out of nowhere and offers to sell us a map that will lead to great riches. And, lo and behold, it just happens to be of the area around the City of Mist." He unfolded his arms and pushed himself up straight on the bench. "The man must have heard us talking back at the Celestial Palace, Sunday, and then decided which of his many maps to try to sell us." He gave a smirk. "Nice little racket he's got going."

"You think the map is a fake."

"I know it's a fake."

She caught the tip of her tongue between her teeth. "I might agree with you, except for one thing."

"What's that?"

"We never spoke of the City of Mist until *after* we'd left the bar. So how did the man know which map to offer us?"

How was he supposed to know? Maybe it had been sheer dumb luck.

If he was smart, Simon realized as he sat there, he would return the woman's deposit now and save them both a whole lot of aggravation.

"I don't know. And frankly I don't care." He got to his feet. "It's time to escort you back to your hotel, Ms. Harrington. You'll want to make an early night of it."

"Why?"

"Because we'll be making an even earlier morning of it tomorrow."

"How early?"

"Six o'clock."

He could tell she wasn't thrilled by the news.

She folded the silk fan and returned it to her handbag, along with the map. "I assume—" she sniffed
"—you mean I should request a six o'clock wake-up
call."

"Nope."

Her head came up. "I have to be ready at six?"

"Ready and waiting outside your hotel with the one
suitcase you're allowed to bring along."

That definitely got her attention. "*One* suitcase?"

Simon realized he was almost enjoying himself.
"And you'd better be able to carry it, yourself. There
won't be any porters handy where we're going. By the
way," he asked as he hailed a passing *samlor*, "what
hotel are you staying at?"

"The Regent."

He should have known. "Only the best, huh?"

"Only the best," she said, as if she was measuring
out her words.

A half hour later, the taxicab pulled up in front of
the most luxurious hotel in Bangkok. As she stepped
from the small three-wheeled vehicle, it finally dawned
on Simon where he had seen Sunday Harrington before. He snapped his fingers together. "Now I know."

She hesitated, and glanced back over her shoulder
at him. "Now you know *what?*"

"Where I've seen you before." The details came to
him. About seven years ago. Her likeness, purple bikini and all, had been splashed across every newspa-
per, television show and billboard, nationwide. Record
sales had been set. For a week or two, there had been

talk of little else. "The cover of *Sports Illustrated,* swimsuit edition."

"You have a good memory for faces," Sunday said as she disappeared into the Regent.

It wasn't only her face that Simon remembered.

Four

The past had caught up with her.

Sooner or later, it always did. She just hadn't expected it to be here or now.

She hadn't expected it to be Simon Hazard.

She refused to apologize, of course, for what she'd done, what she'd been. And she didn't explain. There was no reason to. She'd had an incredibly successful career as a model, and for that she would always be thankful.

But she was not a "babe," and she was not a "bimbo." She was not a body and a face without a brain. She was not a piece of meat. She was not a "loose woman."

She was a talented designer, a business owner and a mature woman of thirty. Yet, to most people—men, in particular—she would always be the girl in the sexy purple bikini.

"That darn swimsuit is going to haunt me forever," Sunday muttered under her breath as she crossed the lobby of the Regent and headed for the elevators.

Simon Hazard was right about one thing: she had been an ugly duckling. Gangly, buck-toothed, freckled, self-conscious, awkward and uncoordinated— that described her perfectly at the age of fifteen.

At sixteen, miraculously, she'd blossomed. As a result, she had signed a lucrative contract with the biggest modeling agency in New York. While everyone else in her high school class back in Cincinnati was worrying about what to wear to the prom, Sunday had been in Paris, modeling haute couture for the most expensive and prestigious French designers. She had gone full steam ahead from that day on, and she'd never looked back.

Not once.

From the beginning, she'd insisted on wearing only three colors: pink, purple or red. The look became her trademark, and was soon heralded as one of the cleverest marketing tools in the industry.

At the age of twenty, she'd graced the covers of every major fashion publication from *Elle* to *Vogue*. She had been making the incredible sum of fifty thousand dollars a day.

At twenty-two, she'd been chosen to appear on the cover of the annual swimsuit edition of *Sports Illustrated*. Sunday and her tiny bikini would go down in history. It became the most talked-about and the bestselling edition of the magazine, ever. For a while, no matter where she turned, Sunday saw herself in those three ridiculously tiny triangles of purple spandex.

She'd gone into modeling with her eyes wide open, but she hadn't counted on the insatiable appetite of the paparazzi and the tabloid press. Any supermodel-cum-celebrity was considered fair game by one and all. Without her consent—even without her knowledge—her life became an open book. One reporter had tracked down some of her former classmates from high school. After all, inquiring minds had wanted to know.

"Sunday Harrington? We called her The Giraffe."

"Sunday Harrington? Isn't she dating some rock star now?"

"Of course, I know Sunday Harrington. We've been the best of friends since the third grade," declared a girl whose name Sunday didn't even recall.

"Sunday was in love with me for years. Probably still is," claimed Brad Peterson, captain of the football team, whose glory days had ended with graduation.

Enough was enough. At twenty-three she had retired.

"So much for my fifteen minutes of fame," Sunday said to herself as the elevator doors closed behind her.

Out of sight, out of mind. That's what she'd asked for and that's what she'd gotten for five years. Although enough of the fickle public remembered her name, her face, her penchant for pink, purple and red for her to make the transition from ex-model to fashion designer two years ago after finally graduating from college.

Only the most exclusive department stores carried Sunday's upscale, expensive line of signature items. She did a little bit of everything from jewelry to belts, from scarves to handbags. All in pink, purple or red. All imprinted with her initials: a stylized, intertwining S and H.

In fact, it was her fashion design business that had brought her to Thailand. She was going to look into doing something with silk for the first time, and where better to learn about silk than in the country where the textile industry had been revolutionized by another American. Before his mysterious disappearance over a quarter of a century ago, Jim Thompson had made Thai silk famous.

When she opened the door of her suite, a welcome blast of cool air hit Sunday square in the face. She closed the door behind her, turned the lock and went straight through to the bedroom. Dropping her handbag onto the dressing table, she kicked off her sandals, slipped out of her silk shirt and pants and stretched out on top of the bed covers. She was hot and tired and hungry, but dinner could wait. A nap was at the top of her list.

Sleep did not come easily; niggling thoughts did.

What was she doing half a world away from home? And what was she doing about to head up into the rugged mountains of northern Thailand with a two-bit cowboy?

But she knew the answers to her own questions. She was on the job. She was searching for inspiration and direction as a designer. Besides, Simon Hazard wasn't really a two-bit cowboy. He was an enigma. He was certainly different from the men she usually met.

Despite her age—her thirtieth birthday had been several months ago—and despite the reputation fostered in the gossip columns, Sunday's experience with the male of the species was far more limited than anyone would guess.

At first she'd been too young, too unattractive and too self-conscious. Then she'd been too famous and too well chaperoned. Plus, the men of her acquaintance seemed to be either married photographers on the make, or effeminate designers who weren't.

Now she was too successful.

And too old.

"You're only as old as you feel," Sunday muttered as she put her head down on the pillow. "Which, at the moment, is somewhere between ninety-five and one hundred."

For some time, she drifted between wakefulness and sleep. Often, her best ideas occurred to her when she was in that twilight state. This afternoon was no exception. Images came and went. Saffron-robed monks. The scent of exotic incense. Golden Buddhas and teak forests, mangoes and creamy coconut-milk sauces. Great carved elephants. Hot and sour, sweet and salty foods. Classical Thai dancers with their elaborate headdresses, bare feet and long nails. Wind chimes and tinkling bells and brass cymbals. Golden spires and mirrored pagodas. Bamboo. Brown rivers. Black panthers.

Sights, sounds, smells, impressions sifted through Sunday's mind. And somewhere in the middle of it all, she found what she was looking for. She would design a whole collection in silk. The colors would be the colors of Thailand: brown, green and, of course, saffron. She would call the collection *Siam.*

The past had finally caught up with him.

Sooner or later, he'd known it would. He just hadn't expected it to be here and now.

He hadn't expected it to be Simon Hazard.

Somebody back at headquarters had made a botch of it. He'd only been informed a month ago that another Hazard—Jonathan was just one of many, it seemed—was in Thailand. Since then, he'd been doing his homework on the man.

What he had found out about Simon Hazard didn't make any sense. The bloke was a millionaire. He had his own company, his own penthouse apartment, even his own tropical island. Why would a man like that be in Thailand driving a bunch of bloody tourists around in a beat-up Range Rover?

Unless Simon Hazard was here to settle an old debt.

He took a last puff on his unfiltered cigarette, removed it from the carved ivory holder—it had been purchased at a night market long before it had become politically incorrect *and* illegal to buy ivory—and disposed of the butt in the ashtray at his elbow.

Now there seemed to be a woman involved, some kind of fashion model or designer.

He had briefly entertained the notion that Sunday Harrington might be in the "business." After all, she did a great deal of traveling, and she had the perfect cover. There was just one flaw in his theory: she was too conspicuous. In fact, with her height, her hair, her eyes, she stuck out like a sore thumb.

He permitted himself a small sigh. This could get messy. There were too many people involved. There was too great a chance of exposure. The whole thing made him damnably nervous.

He didn't like being nervous.

He supposed he had only himself to blame, of course. He'd made a muck of it with Jonathan Hazard back in the old days. He'd left him for dead. He'd assumed the man had drowned in the Chao Phraya River—any other mortal would have.

Unfortunately, Jonathan Hazard had survived. He'd lived to tell the tale. And now, nearly eight years later, another Hazard had turned up in Bangkok, Krung Thep.

"A table for one, sir?" inquired the maître d' at the door of the exclusive Bangkok restaurant.

"Yes. A table for one for tea," he said, looking around the swank room of subdued silk and teakwood, linen and fine china.

He'd always preferred traveling first-class. He liked first-class hotels and first-class restaurants and first-class women. And he wasn't about to allow anyone to ruin it for him now.

If he had to, he would dispose of both Simon Hazard and the Harrington woman. Only this time, he wouldn't botch the job. This time, he would see it through to the end.

Five

The next morning, Simon pulled up in front of the Regent at six o'clock sharp. Sunday Harrington was waiting, one small, soft-sided piece of luggage beside her. She was wearing a simple red dress, a red silk scarf, the same handbag, the same dark glasses and the same expensive leather sandals she'd had on yesterday.

She looked like a million bucks.

"I've got to admit the lady has style," Simon muttered under his breath as he opened the door of the Range Rover and climbed out. "Morning," he said succinctly.

"Yes, it is," she replied with an elegant but unaffected toss of her red hair.

"You're punctual," he observed.

From behind her sunglasses, she shot him a glance.
"I didn't think I had any choice."

He reached for her suitcase. "You didn't." Then he
added, "You don't."

She followed him around to the back of the vehicle. "I assumed if I wasn't ready and waiting, you'd
leave without me."

"You assumed correctly," Simon said, stowing her
suitcase in the rear. He turned, gave her the once-over
and then made a pointed gesture with his hand. "This
outfit is very..."

She volunteered, "Red?"

"Actually, I was going to say impractical." He
folded his arms across his chest and leaned back
against the side of the Rover. "Jeans would have been
a better choice."

He watched as a flicker of annoyance came and
went on her face. "We're still in the city. Besides, the
jeans are in my bag," she informed him.

"And a sensible sweater."

"Also in my bag."

He cocked an eyebrow. "A pair of sturdy walking
shoes."

She was beginning to sound like a broken record.
"In my bag."

He issued one more challenge. "A waterproof
windbreaker."

They concluded in unison: "In my bag."

"I'm not quite the airhead you give me credit for
being, Mr. Hazard," Sunday retorted on a cool note.

So, they were back to *Mr.* Hazard, were they?

"You'll be sitting up front with me." He opened the

passenger door for her, just to show he hadn't completely forgotten his manners.

"Thank you," she said as she slipped by him into the front seat of the Range Rover.

Simon left the parking lot of the Regent, and was soon embroiled in Bangkok's infamous ten-lane traffic. One car after another darted in front of them, horns blaring, drivers shouting, tires squealing, exhaust fumes spewing.

He decided to try to make conversation over the din. After clearing his throat, he announced, "Bangkok is sinking."

One brilliant red eyebrow appeared over the rim of sleek designer sunglasses.

Maybe he should explain. "Bangkok is called the Venice of the East, and like its namesake, it's literally sinking. In some places at the rate of five inches per year." With one hand on the steering wheel, Simon removed his USN cap, combed his fingers through the hair at his nape and replaced his cap. "Most experts blame the problem on the construction of high-rise buildings on what was originally landfill, and the unchecked pumping of underground water. There are also hundreds of miles of canals and periodic flooding of the delta lowlands."

"Perhaps it's a good thing we're leaving town, then," Sunday commented, tongue in cheek.

Without warning, a vintage pickup shot in front of them. The driver slammed on the brakes, opened the door, climbed down from the cab and blithely began to unload boxes from the rear.

"Bananas!" muttered Simon, his foot pressing the brake pedal to the floor.

"Bananas?" echoed Sunday.

He nodded. "Bananas. Mangoes. Breadfruit. Star apples. All on the way to market." He released the brake, maneuvered around the truck and cut back into the melee.

Simon noticed, by this time, that his passenger was sitting with her back ramrod straight. Her hands were folded together in her lap, and she was intermittently wetting her lips with her tongue. The lady wasn't always unflappable, it seemed.

"You're a brave man," she finally said.

Simon knew what she was thinking. "Or maybe just crazy?"

"You're either very brave or very crazy for driving in this traffic," she said with utter honesty. She drew a deep breath and let it out slowly. "How do you do it?"

"No guts, no glory." Simon clicked on the turn signal, leaned on the horn, stuck his head out of the window on the driver's side, held up his hand to stop the *samlor* behind them and gunned it across two lanes of jammed thoroughfare to the exit.

Beside him, he thought he heard a soft gasp. Out of the corner of his eye, he saw Sunday digging her teeth into her bottom lip.

"I'm serious," she said after a time. "How do you drive in *this?*"

He checked the rearview mirror and took the first left. "I told you—"

"No guts, no glory," Sunday repeated. Then she gave a funny little laugh. "And I thought it was madness to drive in New York City."

"'We are all born mad. Some remain so,'" Simon said, mostly to himself.

She finally smiled. "That's right. You have a saying for every occasion, don't you?"

"Just about."

He drove in silence for five minutes. Then he turned down a narrow alley and swung into the parking lot behind a church.

Sunday craned her neck. "What do you call this?"

He put the Range Rover in Park and turned off the ignition. "Our next stop."

She reached up and removed her sunglasses. "Where are we?"

"St. Agnes's," he answered.

Her next question was strictly rhetorical. "There's a Catholic church in the middle of Bangkok?"

Obviously there was. "And a convent. And a medical clinic run by the sisters of St. Agnes. They're affectionately called 'Aggies' for short," Simon told her.

The red silk scarf looped around Sunday's neck had been blown askew. She took a moment to straighten it, and then inquired, "Do you mind if I ask why we're stopping here?"

"I have to pick up something for delivery in Chiang Mai." Simon quickly reassured her, "Don't worry, it's directly on our way to Mae Hong Son."

"Mae Hong Son—the City of Mist," Sunday repeated in a faraway voice. "And, for your information, I wasn't worried."

"Good, because they're badly needed medical supplies for the clinic the Sisters of St. Agnes operate in northern Thailand." He pointed to the seat beneath them. "You stay here and keep an eye on things. I'll be right back."

When Simon returned ten minutes later, she didn't appear to have moved a muscle. He'd never seen a woman less likely to fidget. Maybe it was a result of her years posing in front of the cameras. Or maybe she was simply a sea of calm amidst the general chaos of life.

The box of medical supplies was unwieldy; it was also getting heavy. Sunday must have realized he could use a hand. She opened her door and jumped down from the Range Rover.

"Thanks. In the back," he said.

He shoved the crate between her one small bag and his knapsack, making sure it wouldn't slide around any more than was necessary—at least not until he had the other passengers' luggage in place—and shut the rear door.

That's when a cool, calm and slightly accented female voice said from nearby, "Thank you, Simon. I don't know what we would do without you."

He turned. "You're welcome, Mother Superior."

Sunday tried not to stare, but the woman speaking to Simon was beautiful. Perhaps one of the most beautiful women she'd ever set eyes on—and she'd seen hundreds, maybe thousands, in her professional life.

Tall, stately, ageless and graceful, the woman Simon had addressed as Mother Superior was dressed in a traditional flowing white habit. There was a plain gold cross on a chain around her neck and a bunch of keys dangling from her waist. Her wimple was large, white and starched; it was straight out of "The Flying Nun."

"And who might this be?" she inquired, not unkindly.

Simon made the appropriate introductions. When he was finished, the woman bestowed a warm smile on her. "*Sawat-dii!* Greetings! Welcome to Thailand, Miss Harrington."

"Thank you, Mother Superior."

"I understand you are journeying to the north with Simon."

Sunday nodded. "Yes, I am."

"You have chosen well."

She certainly hoped so.

"We'd better be on our way," Simon interjected. "I have several more stops to make this morning, and I'd like to be out of the city before the heat of the day."

Mother Superior folded her hands in front of her and nodded knowingly. "In that case, I will just be one moment." She quickly disappeared behind the doors of the convent.

Simon turned to her and said with a slightly mystified shrug, "Mother Superior must have forgotten the mail. Sometimes I deliver letters to the sisters in Chiang Mai as well as supplies."

Sunday glanced over his shoulder. "I don't think it's the mail," she said in a discreet whisper.

It was a second nun. She was carrying a battered valise in her right hand and an equally battered umbrella in her left. She was small and young. Her plain white habit was identical to the one worn by the Mother Superior, except she carried no keys at her waist.

The older woman raised her hand, made the sign of the cross and recited a blessing. "May the good Lord be with you on your journey, Sister."

"Thank you, *Mater*," she murmured.

Then the religious superior of St. Agnes turned to them. "God's blessings and a safe journey to you all." With that, she disappeared into the convent. The thick, teakwood door shut behind her with resounding finality.

The young nun looked from one to the other—she seemed to realize she was a total surprise to both of them—and said apologetically, "Mother Superior forgot to tell you about me, didn't she? I'm sure she meant to. I'm certain she thought she had. It's just that she's had so much on her mind lately, so many duties and responsibilities."

Sunday stepped forward and said reassuringly, "There's no need to worry, Sister. We'll get along swimmingly. I'm Sunday Harrington, another of Mr. Hazard's passengers."

The young woman in the white habit returned a tentative smile. "I'm afraid I don't know how to swim, Miss Harrington, but my name is Sister Agatha Anne."

Simon reached for the young nun's valise and stowed it in the back, while she settled Sister Agatha Anne in the Range Rover.

The newcomer inquired in a sweet and curious voice, "Is your christened name really Sunday?"

"Yes, it is."

"And were you truly born on the Sabbath?"

"I was."

"'A child that's born on the Sabbath day is fair and wise and good and gay.'" Then Sister Agatha Anne blushed. "Gay meaning happy or exuberant, of course."

"Of course," said Sunday.

"I have been blessed with my names, as well. Our order—the Sisters of St. Agatha—was named in honor of the third-century martyr. St. Anne was the name of the mother of the Virgin Mary."

Once they were all settled, Sunday turned to him. "I wonder what the name Simon means."

The answer came from the seat behind them. "Simon means 'one who hears.'"

"Right now, it means 'one who speaks,'" he informed them. "Please make sure you have your seat belts fastened. We will be making a mad dash across town to pick up the Grimwades."

"The Grimwades?" There were more people joining them? "Who, pray tell, are the Grimwades?"

Three-quarters of an hour later, she had her answer as the Grimwades joined the expedition. They were a young Australian couple touring Thailand and Malaysia.

"We're off to see the world before we're too old to appreciate it, don't you see?" offered Nigel Grimwade, a slender young man with slender blond hair who kept one arm around his slender young wife at all times.

"We've never been anywhere but Australia until now," explained Millicent Grimwade. "You're both Americans, aren't you?" she said from the back seat.

Sunday turned her head. "Yes, we are."

Nigel Grimwade spoke up. "Millie and I want to visit the States one day. Don't we, sweets?"

She nodded. "Walt Disney World."

"Epcot," he added.

"Sea World." Millie Grimwade opened her handbag, took out a crumpled tissue and began to clean her eyeglasses with it. "Have you been lots of places, Miss Harrington?"

"A few."

"You could be a model."

It was an innocent enough comment. In fact, it was, in all likelihood, meant to be a compliment. But there was something about Millicent Grimwade...

The Australian woman put on her glasses, blew her nose on the tissue, stuffed the crumpled hanky back into her handbag and went on, "I mean, you're tall and slender, and you're a looker."

"Thank you," Sunday said, not knowing how else to respond.

The young Mrs. Grimwade persisted. "Have you done any modeling?"

"A little. When I was younger." Sunday heard the man beside her snicker softly.

The next time Millicent Grimwade opened her mouth, she put her slender foot in it. "I suppose when a woman reaches a *certain* age, she's considered to be over the hill when it comes to a modeling career. What do you do now?"

Sunday gritted her teeth and replied, "I'm a fashion designer." She declined to mention that many models were still going strong in their thirties, and even in their forties and beyond. Mrs. Grimwade looked as if she was barely out of her teens.

Thankfully, at that point, the visiting Australian couple struck up a conversation with Sister Agatha Anne.

Sunday leaned toward Simon, and dropping her voice, asked, "Are we picking up any more passengers, Mr. Hazard?"

"Just one."

She studied his profile. He had rather nice ears. They weren't too big and they weren't too small for the rest of his features, and they were nicely tucked against his head. For some incredible reason—maybe the heat and humidity had taken a greater toll on her than she'd realized—Sunday had an inexplicable urge to blow in Simon Hazard's ear, just to see what he would do.

She gave herself a good shake. "Just one?"

He kept his eyes straight ahead on the road. "Colonel Arthur Bantry."

"You're going to have a full load," she observed.

"A bit fuller than I'd expected," he said for her ears only. "Sister Agatha Anne was a complete surprise, and the Colonel signed on just last evening."

"I suppose we could tell ourselves the more the merrier," Sunday said philosophically, lifting the weight of her hair off her neck and shoulders. She wished she'd taken the time to braid it this morning.

"I suppose we could," Simon said, not sounding convinced.

She laughed lightly. "I feel like I'm in one of those Agatha Christie novels where a group of colorful characters meet on a train or a plane or a boat, and someone is mysteriously murdered."

"And everybody becomes a suspect."

"But, contrary to popular opinion, it's not the butler."

"And it's never the faithful, overworked, underpaid guide."

She arched a teasing eyebrow. "Are you certain?"

"I'm positive." Simon shot her a quick sideways glance. "I believe the culprit was a model once, however."

Sunday shook her head. "Impossible." She shrugged and allowed, "Well, improbable, anyway." She glanced down at the space between them. She'd have to scoot over to make room for the Colonel, which would practically put her in Simon Hazard's lap. "We're going to be packed in like sardines."

Simon reached over and patted her hand reassuringly. "Don't worry. No one is allowed to kill anyone else in this vehicle, no matter how crowded it gets. That's one of my primary rules."

With that, he pulled up in front of another luxury hotel. A gentleman with perfect posture, wearing a neatly pressed quasi-military jacket—there were epaulets at the shoulders and brass buttons down the front—was standing at attention on the front steps. A small leather satchel sat at his feet. His shoes had a spit and polish to them. He was leaning on a brass-tipped walking stick.

"Colonel Bantry?"

"Indeed. And you must be Mr. Hazard."

Simon nodded. "I'll take your bag."

"I can manage. Thanks all the same, old chap." The militarylike satchel was quickly stored with the rest of the luggage in the back of the vehicle.

"I'll introduce you to your fellow passengers now," Sunday heard Simon say to the very proper British gentleman as he joined them in the front seat of the Range Rover.

Sunday watched and she listened. She made the appropriate responses when it was required of her, but something kept niggling at her. Bits and pieces of a conversation she'd had yesterday with Simon ran and reran in her head.

"Everything isn't always what it seems to be," she had said as they sat outside the Temple of the Reclining Buddha.

"Or everyone," he had tacked on.

There was something about these people, she realized. Something odd. Something she couldn't quite put her finger on.

It was the darnedest thing.

It was almost as if not one of them was really *who* or *what* they claimed to be....

Six

She took it back.

After traveling with them for four days in Simon's beat-up Range Rover, joggling over bumpy roads, dodging lunatic Thai truck drivers, eating only what came with a skin they could peel, rationing their bottled water, sleeping in countryside inns, sometimes using primitive bathrooms, sometimes making do with the privacy provided by a *Ficus elastica,* the tropical Asian rubber plant, Sunday decided these people were exactly what they seemed to be.

Sister Agatha Anne was quiet and rather sweet. She occasionally chatted with one of them, but most of the time she had her nose stuck in a book titled *The Nun's Way.*

The Grimwades did not wear nearly as well. The pair were immature, brash, overbearing and cloyingly affectionate with each other. They talked loudly and incessantly.

The Colonel was another matter altogether. He was very polite, very proper, very courteous, very everything, including very British.

But it was Simon who surprised Sunday the most. She'd expected him to be nothing but trouble with a capital T. Instead, he'd displayed a genuine ability to deal with people. He was diplomatic, patient, good-humored and a born leader.

"*Scroop* is the technical term used to describe the rustling sound made by silk fabrics," Sunday said to the Colonel, continuing a conversation they had begun after lunch.

It was Colonel Bantry's turn to volunteer an obscure fact. He thought for a moment and said to her, "The bite of a king cobra can kill an elephant."

"Yes, I know." She wondered if Simon was listening.

The gentleman beside her tried again. "An elephant can sprint up to speeds of twenty-five miles per hour."

She hadn't realized that. "If what you've said is true, a man can't outrun an elephant."

He fingered his moustache. "Quite."

"I told you," Simon interjected in a sardonic tone of voice, "the first rule of the forest is—"

"Never take an elephant for granted," she finished for him.

There was a flash of white teeth. "You remembered."

"I remembered."

"All right, people, listen up," Simon said. "The road we have to take to Lamphun, then to Chiang Mai and, for those traveling on, from Chiang Mai to Mae Hong Son, is steep, narrow and occasionally, during the rainy season, treacherous."

This was the rainy season, Sunday recalled. Simon had told her so, himself.

"Lately, there have been a few . . . incidents."

"Incidents?" Sunday suddenly felt the tiny hairs on the back of her neck stand straight on end. "What kind of incidents?"

Simon explained for everyone's benefit, "Every now and then, the Union of Myanmar army stages a border raid between Thailand and what was once known as Burma. Or a bandit sticks up a traveler for his wristwatch and a few *baht*. There's nothing to be concerned about. We'll take a few simple precautions, that's all."

Sunday was becoming uneasier by the minute. "Precautions?"

"We don't flash any money or jewelry around in public. We don't stop unless we absolutely have to." His lips thinned. "And if we do, *I* do the talking."

"I assume," Sunday said after a lull in the conversation, "a 'call of nature' falls under the heading of 'absolutely have to.'"

Simon shifted the Range Rover into low gear as they started their ascent of the mountain track. "We'll take a short 'necessary' break—and I do mean short—

every two hours." He glanced in the rearview mirror at the trio behind them. "Any questions?"

"Not a one, mate," said Nigel Grimwade agreeably.

"Does everyone understand?"

They all nodded.

"You must have dealt with a number of perilous situations in your time, Colonel," Simon said, without taking his eyes off the road. "Do you have anything to add?"

The Brit shook his head from side to side. "There is an old saying, Mr. Hazard."

They waited to hear what it was.

Colonel Bantry stroked his moustache in what Sunday recognized was a habitually nervous gesture. "'Wise men say nothing in dangerous times.'"

She gave a sigh. "Another proverb."

"It's from the writings of John Selden, a seventeenth-century English jurist and antiquary," he expounded, bestowing upon her the closest thing to a smile she had seen from him.

A masculine voice came from the back seat. "Jurist?"

The Colonel sat up very straight. "Solicitor. Barrister. Lawyer."

Millicent Grimwade was apparently cut from the same cloth as her husband. "What's an antiquary?" she inquired.

"It usually means someone who's interested in old or rare books, but it can refer to a collector or a student of any type of antiquities," Arthur Bantry said, tapping his walking stick against a highly polished shoe. Even after four days on the road, his appearance was impeccable.

The young Australian woman guffawed. Her laugh was always too loud and too shrill. "Lordy, mate, you do know a lot of stuff. What's your sheila say about it, hey?"

After clearing his throat, Arthur Bantry remarked to no one in particular, "I'm not married."

Millicent laughed again and whispered loudly to her husband, "I'm not surprised."

"Selden also expressed his thoughts about matrimony, and I find I quite agree with him," the Colonel went on. "He wrote in his *Table Talks*—'Marriage is a desperate thing.'"

A thin furrow appeared on Millicent Grimwade's otherwise wrinkle-free face. "I don't get it."

The British gentleman put his nose a notch higher and said with a polite sniff, "I'm not surprised."

Simon apparently decided it was time to divert the company's attention to other matters. "If you will look at the large tree on the left side of the vehicle," he directed, "you may be lucky enough to catch a glimpse of the rare and exotic bird, *Rupicola peruviana,* commonly called cock-of-the-rock."

"Cock-of-the-rock?" he heard Sunday repeat with a chuckle several hours later as they made their way through the wet underbrush. There had been a recent drenching afternoon rain; it had come down in buckets. "I don't believe any such bird exists."

"Oh, it exists, all right," Simon said as he tramped along behind her. "Primarily in Colombia and Peru, however. I doubt if one has ever been spotted within a thousand miles of Thailand."

"You handled that well, you know," she said to him.

He decided to play dumb. "Handled what well?"

Sunday threw him a glance over her shoulder. "The nasty little contretemps between Mrs. Grimwade and the Colonel."

"Oh, *that*."

"Yes, *that*."

He set his mouth. "I told you, I have my rules."

She snapped her thumb and middle finger together. "That's right. The passengers aren't allowed to kill one another, are they?"

Simon was not amused. It had been a very long four days on the road. "That isn't funny, Sunday. At least not at this point."

"I can see why you might have a tendency to lose your sense of humor on a trip like this," she commiserated.

He felt as though his sense of humor had deserted him some miles back, and he told her so.

"I still don't understand why you have to be the one to keep watch while I use the so-called privacy of the bushes," Sunday said as they hiked a short distance from the Rover.

Simon took in and let out a deep breath before he replied, "Because I'm your guide."

"Why couldn't Sister Agatha Anne, or even Mrs. Grimwade, for that matter, stand guard?" Sunday seemed to reconsider. "Well, perhaps not Millicent Grimwade."

"Sister has wisely decided to stay put in the Range Rover. Mr. Grimwade is accompanying Mrs. Grimwade on a 'necessary' stop in that direction." He pointed to their right. "The Colonel is quite capable of looking after himself. That leaves me—" he pointed first to his own chest and then to hers "—to keep an eye on you. After all, I feel responsible for you as long as you're traveling under my auspices."

There was a soft *humph* from in front of him.

He added for good measure, "Besides, I'm the one with the gun."

Sunday stopped dead in her tracks, pivoted on her heel and gave him a once-over. "Are you really carrying a concealed weapon?"

"As a matter of fact, several," he answered with a perfectly straight face.

She looked briefly disconcerted. "Several?"

Simon leaned over and patted the side of his boot. "Bowie knife. A bon voyage present from my cousin, Mathis, when I left the States. The blade is five inches long and razor sharp."

Green eyes grew round as saucers. "You keep a knife stashed in your cowboy boot?"

Simon grunted. "Yup."

She was curious. "How do you keep from stabbing yourself?" she wanted to know.

"I had a special leather sheath made for it."

Her mouth formed an O.

Next, he dived down the back of his jeans with one hand and brought out his revolver. "A Beretta is small but deadly," he said, double-checking that the safety was on.

Sunday wrapped her arms around herself and seemed to shiver in spite of the tropical heat. "I don't like guns."

Simon put the Beretta away, but not before a very old, and very irreverent, Mae West line popped into his head: *Is that your gun, or are you just glad to see me?*

Sunday planted her hands on her hips—he couldn't help noticing how good she looked in a pair of tight jeans—and tapped her foot in the damp humus on the forest floor. "Why, pray tell, are you grinning from ear to ear?"

Simon only hoped his face, and other parts of his anatomy, didn't give him away. "Can't tell you."

She narrowed her eyes. "Can't or won't?"

"Won't. Too embarrassing." He stopped himself from saying any more.

A splash of pink suddenly appeared on her cheeks. "Speaking of embarrassing, did it ever occur to you that I might find it embarrassing to use the great outdoors as a 'necessary,' with you standing only a few feet away?"

"I'll turn my back." He did so.

"There . . . are other . . . problems," he heard her stammer.

"I'll sing."

And he did, in a slightly off-key but booming baritone. He began with a rousing rendition of "I've Got Plenty of Nothin'" and concluded with "Stranger in Paradise."

He finally felt a tap on his shoulder.

"Thank you," Sunday said politely.

"You're welcome."

She gave him a relieved smile. "You sing very..."

"Beautifully?"

"I was going to say loudly." Then she laughed. Simon realized he liked the sound of her laughter: it was sweet and natural and infectious. "You may have even frightened away the rare and exotic cock-on-the-rock, you know."

"I may have."

As they hiked back to the road, Simon studied the woman beside him. There wasn't a speck of makeup on her face. Her hair was a frizz of curls from the heat and humidity. She had been wearing the same pair of blue jeans and the same red pullover sweater since the day after they'd left Bangkok. And, damn, if she still wasn't the most beautiful and desirable creature he'd ever set eyes on.

She was dangerous.

She was a definite hazard to his peace of mind, to his vow of abstinence, to his best intentions. Traveling with her through Thailand for the next several weeks was going to turn out to be hazardous duty.

In the navy, of course, "hazardous duty" meant a high-risk assignment requiring a sailor with nerves of steel.

A memory of a long, sleek and voluptuous body in a revealing bikini flashed into Simon's mind. Then a new image took shape, an image of his hands replacing those three ridiculously tiny purple triangles covering Sunday's breasts and bottom. Too bad he only had two hands....

He could always use his hands *and* his mouth, came the erotic thought that nearly sent him over the edge.

"That's peculiar," murmured Sunday.

Simon blinked several times in quick succession and forced himself back from his daydreams. "What's peculiar?"

She raised her arm and pointed to a spot visible through the thicket. "That is."

Simon looked to where the Range Rover was parked, then twenty yards ahead to a second vehicle that was blocking the road. He bit off a sharp expletive.

She frowned. "What is it?"

"We have to move and we have to move fast."

She glanced up at him as they broke into a trot. "Simon?"

"Do exactly what I tell you, Sunday."

"You're frightening me."

"Good. I want you to get in the Range Rover with the others and stay there!" he barked.

A word formed on her lips. "Why?"

Simon hoped and prayed he was wrong, but he didn't think so. "Bandits."

Seven

"**B**y the bones of the blessed martyrs, who are those men?" Sister Agatha Anne asked in a frenetic whisper when Sunday jerked open the door on the driver's side of the Range Rover and jumped in, slamming it shut behind her.

"Bandits, I should say," offered Colonel Bantry. "Of course, that's merely conjecture on my part."

Sunday struggled to keep her voice even. "Simon agrees. The last word he said to me was 'bandits.'"

"Ohmigod, we're all going to be killed!" wailed Millicent Grimwade. "We're going to be robbed and beaten and left to die a slow, painful death in this godforsaken place." Then, as if on cue, she burst into tears and buried her face in her husband's shirt.

Sunday didn't mean to be unkind, but histrionics were no help. "Don't be ridiculous," she said brusquely. "No one is going to die."

There was a muffled sob behind her. "How d-do you know?"

"Simon will make certain nothing happens to us," she said clearly and stubbornly.

Arthur Bantry gave her a long, measuring look. "You seem to have a great deal of faith in the man," he observed.

"Simon Hazard knows this country like the back of his hand. He speaks the language fluently. He understands the people and their customs. He's the best," she said with conviction.

"Mother Superior has complete faith in him, too," piped up Sister Agatha Anne as she sat clutching her book.

"I just wish I didn't feel so helpless," Sunday said, mostly to herself. "I wish I had some kind of weapon." She turned to the retired army officer beside her. "Your name is Arthur, isn't it?"

"Yes. Arthur Egbert Bantry. I was named for the legendary kings of England." There was more than a hint of pride in his voice.

"Well, Arthur Egbert Bantry, I wish you had Excalibur with you," she said with a sigh.

"Oh, but I do," he replied, unscrewing the top of his walking stick and withdrawing a small sword; it wasn't much larger than a knife, really. "In the event of an emergency," he said, apparently to explain the reason he was carrying a weapon.

"Good Lord, mate, will you put that thing away before you get us all murdered?" whined Nigel Grimwade.

"Yes, you'd better put it away," said Sunday. "Simon can take care of things if it comes to that."

The Colonel's eyes narrowed. "Is he armed?"

She nodded.

"A revolver?"

"A Beretta down his back, and a bowie knife in his boot." She hastened to reassure everyone, "I'm sure it won't come to a showdown, however."

"It bloody well better not," snarled the Aussie. "Hazard is outnumbered and outgunned."

Sunday watched as Simon conversed with the man who appeared to be the leader of the bandits. The man was wearing a quasi-military hat and seemed more heavily armed than the others. There was a nasty-looking machete dangling at his side, the butt of a revolver appeared above his belt and he had a semiautomatic rifle clasped in his hand. There were two or three men with him, a motley group of no particular size or age.

"I wonder what they're saying," she murmured, peering through the front window.

The conversation was animated. First, one spoke, then the other. Heads were shaken. Occasionally, someone raised an arm and gestured in their direction, or back toward the bandits' truck. They were obviously discussing the vehicle blocking the road.

It started to rain again. Droplets of water ran down the windshield. Sunday didn't dare turn on the ignition to start the wipers, but it was getting more and more difficult to see.

Out of the corner of her eye, she glimpsed a movement in the forest. She took in a breath and held it. More bandits. Three—no, four of them. Young, and armed with machetes and rifles.

Maybe Simon realized they were there, and maybe he didn't. Maybe he could take care of himself...and then again, maybe he couldn't. Maybe he needed a good—and a very tall—woman at his side. The Colonel and Nigel Grimwade were certainly making no move to come to his aid.

"Colonel, you're in charge," Sunday said, scooting over to the door. "If worse comes to worst, take the Range Rover and the other passengers and get the hell out of Dodge City."

"I b-beg your pardon," he stammered.

"Take the others and leave," she said.

Millicent Grimwade sat up straight in her seat and pushed the hair back from her tear-stained face. "W-where are you going?"

"To help Simon."

"Dominus vobiscum," intoned Sister Agatha Anne. "The Lord be with you."

"Thank you, Sister."

Sunday opened the door and got out. She took a deep, fortifying breath, gave herself a quick pep talk and started walking toward the group of men facing Simon on the road.

Damn the woman!

What the hell did she think she was doing? He had

told her to get back in the Rover with the others and stay there. The situation was precarious enough as it was. The head man facing him was negotiating for their safe passage along this stretch of road. The presence of a woman—and Simon was pretty sure none of these bandits had ever seen a woman like Sunday Harrington—was bound to complicate matters.

The brigands were speaking Thai to him and their native dialect to one another—each hill tribe in the north of Thailand had its own language. But he was pretty sure the leader, if not all of the gang members, understood English. There was no way for him to warn Sunday to watch what she said. He could only hope that she would somehow take her cue from him.

"I thought I told you to stay put," Simon muttered out of the side of his mouth as she approached.

Sunday stopped beside him, turned her face up to his and smiled bravely, but he saw the concern in her eyes. "I wondered what was keeping you."

"I've been talking with these men and their leader, Ho."

"Ho?"

"Ho," he said, indicating the small man with the large gun.

Ho. Ho. Ho.

Simon fought a sudden, crazy urge to laugh. This was no laughing matter, he reminded himself. Thank goodness, Sunday didn't crack a smile.

"Are these men having trouble with their truck?" she inquired innocently, looking past them to where the vintage Ford pickup blocked the highway.

"I'll ask them." Simon switched to Thai and inquired, on behalf of the lady present, if something was wrong with their vehicle.

Ho spoke for several minutes, gesturing wildly with one hand and occasionally waving the other—the one with the semiautomatic weapon in it—in the air.

There was a short, brittle pause.

"There is nothing wrong with their truck," Simon relayed to her.

"Then I'm sure these gentlemen will move their pickup so that we may pass by," Sunday said, carefully enunciating each word. "For it is written that a brave man does not make war on women or the innocent."

He'd love to ask her *where* it was written, but this wasn't the time or the place. At least she was clever enough to behave as if the head man understood every word she was saying—which he probably did.

Ho spoke again and Simon responded. Then he turned and translated for Sunday. "The leader of this band of men wants to know if we have any of the poppy with us."

Sunday wrinkled her nose. "The poppy?"

"Opium."

"Opium!"

Simon quickly reassured her. "I've explained that we have no opium."

"Of course, we don't have any opium." Sunday let out a frustrated sigh. "We have nothing but the clothes on our backs. Anyone can see that we're a simple group of travelers, including a holy sister, journeying to Chiang Mai."

One of the other native hill men stepped forward and began to ramble in his native dialect. Then he raised his finger and pointed at Sunday. In turn, Ho posed the question to Simon in Thai. The bandits stood and stared at the woman beside him.

"What is it?" she asked.

"They want to know if your hair is really that color red, or if you dye it with the juice of the elephant-berry plant."

Sunday reached up and patted her head. "Of course, this is the real color of my hair."

Another of the border raiders came closer, grinned a toothless grin and jabbered for half a minute.

"This one is asking if all Americans are as big as we are," Simon eventually interpreted for her.

Sunday pulled herself up to her full height—the woman really was magnificent at times—and looked down the length of her lovely nose. "I wish I knew how to say yes in their language."

"I think they get the message," he said with a touch of irony.

Ho barked a command to his raggedy troops, including the young men who had emerged from the forest, then he circled the pair of them, his eyes never leaving Sunday for a minute. Simon had to admit the guy was making him nervous.

Ho finally spoke. Simon listened intently. Once he understood the bandit's business, his natural instinct was to slip a protective arm around the woman beside him. In fact, that was exactly what he did.

Sunday glanced up at him. "What is it?"

Simon cleared his throat and prepared himself for her reaction. "This man has made an offer for you."

She stiffened. "An offer for me?"

Adrenaline was shooting into Simon's bloodstream. Every one of his senses was on red alert, but he realized the importance of keeping his wits about him and maintaining a poker face. He knew the price they might all pay if he didn't. "I have told the leader Ho that it isn't our custom."

Green eyes darkened to the color of the teakwood forest at sunset. "*What* isn't our custom?"

He knew she would ask. "I cannot sell you."

Sunday was quick to shake her head and even quicker to reply. "You certainly cannot."

Simon drew her closer. He could feel the ripple of surprise and awareness that swept through Sunday as their bodies touched. She fit him perfectly. It was almost as if the size and shape of his leg, his thigh, his waist, even his chest, had been molded to fit hers.

It was the damnedest thing.

For a brief instant, Simon wondered if they would fit perfectly in other ways, as well. Later, he promised himself. If they got out of this mess alive, he would find out later.

"I have explained that in our country, a man does not sell or share—" he dropped the bomb "—his wife."

The expression on Sunday Harrington's face was priceless. It was almost worth the aggravation of the past four days, of dealing with the likes of the Grimwades, of standing out in the pouring rain getting soaked to the skin, of encountering a gang of cut-throats.

"W-wife?" Sunday stumbled over the word.

Simon added after a brief pause, "Besides, you are worth far more than two pigs."

Her mouth opened and closed several times, before she managed to sputter, "Two pigs?"

"Indeed, I've told Ho that in America, a woman such as yourself brings a great dowry of many pigs, many water buffalo and many fine sheep to her marriage," he elaborated.

He was right about one thing: the bandit who called himself Ho understood English. He stopped Simon and questioned him about what kind of sheep were raised in America. Were they similar to their own mountain goats?

To make matters worse—he hadn't thought it was possible—it began to pour. The rain came down in sheets, plastering their clothes to their bodies. Sunday's sweater and jeans soon clung to her in a most revealing fashion.

"I'm soaked through," Sunday announced to the assemblage as if she were the Queen of Sheba. "We must return to our vehicle and continue our journey to Chiang Mai." Then she shivered and wrapped her arms around herself.

"You're cold, *darling,*" Simon said, drawing her closer.

Her teeth began to chatter in earnest. "I'm freezing, *darling.*"

Ho made a dismissing gesture with his hand and finally announced in Thai, "You may go."

Simon wasn't one to usually question his good luck, but he found he had to know. "Why are you allowing us to pass?"

Lowering his semiautomatic rifle, Ho smiled an inscrutable smile and said in Thai, "The lady is correct. A brave man does not make war on women and innocents." Then he ordered his men to move their truck.

"Thank you," Simon said politely in the same language.

Ho walked away with a bandit's swagger. Then he stopped and peered back over his shoulder. "Are you certain you will not take three pigs for the woman?"

Simon responded in the same language, "It is a most generous offer, but I cannot part with her." He shrugged. "She has bewitched me."

"This is a rare female," the bandit observed.

"Rare, indeed." Then Simon turned and, without a backward glance, urged Sunday toward the Range Rover.

"What did he say?" she whispered.

"He said we can go."

"And?"

He kept his arm around her shoulders and hurried her along. "And he upped his offer to three pigs."

Sunday glared at him.

"Don't worry. I turned him down flat."

"Very funny," she snapped, wiping the rain from her eyes. "By the way, you can thank me anytime."

Simon frowned. "Thank you for what?"

She gave him a look that was rich with meaning. "For saving your precious hide, cowboy."

"Good grief, surely you don't think—"

"I certainly do."

He wasn't about to let Sunday Harrington assume she'd saved his rear, or any other part of him, for that matter. Once a woman got that kind of hold over a man, she never let him forget it.

"I was doing fine until you interfered."

"Really?"

"Yes. Really." He took in a deep breath and slowly let it out again. "You went against my orders. I told you to stay put."

"I thought it might help to create a diversion," she said.

"Help?" Simon realized he had the strongest urge to either choke her or kiss her. Maybe both. "Is that what you call it?"

"Well, what do you call it?" she challenged.

"Stupidity."

"It wasn't stupidity," Sunday retorted. "You were one against—" she counted on her fingers "—seven or eight."

"So you thought you'd improve the odds?"

She sunk her teeth into her lower lip. "Something like that."

Simon stopped dead in his tracks and faced her. "So, by virtue of your height, your red hair and your green eyes, you thought to create a diversion and, somehow, rescue me from seven or eight men armed with machetes and semiautomatic rifles?"

"When you put it like that," she allowed, "it sounds idiotic."

"It sounds idiotic because it is bloody idiotic!"

Sunday blinked several times in quick succession. "Why are you yelling at me?"

Was he yelling?

He was. "Because I'm mad. Because you scared the living sh—daylights out of me back there." He brought his hand up to cup her chin. "Because I want to kiss you so bad I can taste it, and I can't because we have an audience watching every move we make."

Sunday stood there in the pouring rain and gazed up at him.

Simon shook his head and brushed the strands of dripping hair away from her face. "You crazy little fool."

She smiled tremulously. "Maybe. But I'll tell you the same thing I told Colonel Bantry."

"What's that?"

"Let's get the hell out of Dodge City."

"I couldn't have said it better, myself," Simon admitted as they made a dash for the Range Rover.

Eight

"Like rats deserting a sinking ship," Sunday grumbled to herself as she left her hotel room to meet Simon.

It had been several days since the incident involving the armed bandits on the road. She was rested, refreshed, *dry* and ready to visit Chiang Mai's famous night market.

Apparently, she was the only one.

The same evening they had reached the northern Thai city, Millicent and Nigel Grimwade had jumped ship. They hadn't even bothered to change their clothes or stay for the night in the hotel accommodations Simon had arranged for them. In fact, the young Australian couple had insisted upon being dropped off at the airport so they could hire a charter flight to take them back to Bangkok.

"Good riddance," Sunday muttered, swinging her leather handbag over the shoulder of her red dress.

Sister Agatha Anne, of course, had reached her intended destination with their arrival in Chiang Mai. She had gone directly to the clinic run by the Sisters of St. Agnes, along with the crate of medical supplies.

Even Colonel Bantry had abruptly changed his plans. He'd made the announcement only this morning at breakfast. He'd run into an old school chum from his days at Harrow, someone he referred to as "Bunky." Anyway, Arthur Bantry had decided to remain with his friend rather than continue with them to the City of Mist.

"Like rats from a sinking ship," Sunday repeated as she walked toward the front lobby of the modest hotel.

After all, Simon had to make a living, too. No doubt he had counted on the fares that he would be paid for driving the Grimwades and the Colonel for the next several weeks. Instead, she was going to be his only passenger.

Money was the problem. She had a lot of it, and Simon had very little.

"How can I broach this delicate subject without damaging his sizable male ego?" she pondered aloud.

"Whose sizable male ego?" came a familiar masculine voice from behind her.

Her face heated. She turned around. "Simon."

"Sunday." His eyebrows drew together in a classic frown. "*What* delicate subject and *whose* sizable male ego?" he repeated.

She dismissed the whole business offhandedly. "It was nothing."

"Nothing?" His tone was one of disbelief. "Somehow, I think it must have been *something*." He gently scolded her. "After all we've been through together in the past week, this is no time to start having secrets from each other."

She wanted to have her secrets. She didn't want him to read her mind or know her every thought. Good grief, some of her thoughts had been rather private and very personal!

The truth was, Simon Hazard made her nervous. He made her self-conscious, and aware of him in a way that no other man ever had.

He put his hand on her shoulder with apparent casualness. "Sunday—?"

"Money," she blurted out.

He looked baffled. "Money?"

She swiftly nodded her head. "Dollars. Francs. Rupees. Deutsche marks. *Bahts*."

"I think I get the idea. What about money?"

She stifled a sigh. "I'm worried you won't have enough."

"Enough for what?"

Sunday wet her lips with her tongue and drew in a deep breath. "Things."

He appeared puzzled. "What kind of things?"

"Food. Gas. Lodging."

"You're starting to sound like an exit sign on the expressway," he said dryly.

She cleared her throat. "I know you must have been counting on the fares from the Grimwades and Colonel Bantry, and now that they've up and left you high and dry—"

"Good riddance... at least to the Grimwades," he said, echoing her sentiments. "I didn't mind the Colonel. He was a bit stiff, but that type usually is."

Sunday gave him a speculative glance. "But you won't get paid," she told him.

"Nope."

"You don't seem worried about it."

"I'm not." He paused, then added, "You know what they say about money."

"It's the root of all evil?" she ventured.

"Actually, the original quotation was, '*love* of money is the root of all evil,'" he said, correcting her. "My personal motto is easy come, easy go."

Sunday stopped, turned toward him and planted her hands on her hips. "That's all you have to say after what you've been through this week—Easy come, easy go?"

"It's only money, Sunday," he stated, shrugging his shoulders. "Besides, if there's one thing I've learned as a tour guide, it's to expect the unexpected."

Speaking of the unexpected, there was something different about Simon tonight. Sunday finally figured out what it was. "You're not wearing your USN cap."

Simon combed his fingers through soft black curls and expressed aloud what she'd known all along. "I need a haircut."

"Surely they have barbers in Chiang Mai."

"They do. But the barbers here only know one way to cut hair." The flicker of a smile came and went. "I'm afraid I'll end up looking like a monk."

"No matter what was done to your hair, you wouldn't look like a monk," she blurted out as they continued on their way.

"Remind me to ask you later what you mean by that," he said as they reached the lobby and the street beyond. "Are you ready to shop till you drop?"

"I'm ready."

"Then we're off."

Once they'd reached the entrance to the marketplace, which had booths and makeshift stalls lining both sides of the narrow, ancient street, Simon issued a warning. "If the price seems too good to be true, it probably is. This place is infamous, for its five-dollar Rolex watches, 'instant' antiques and cheap designer clothes."

"Forewarned is forearmed," she replied.

The night bazaar of Chiang Mai was another world altogether: a world of glowing brass lanterns, of exotic fruits and flowers, of embroidered cloth and wall hangings depicting fierce dragons, rare birds and the now-extinct Chinese tiger, of pungent odors wafting from open-air food stalls, of people jabbering in languages Sunday had never heard before, of squawking chickens and bleating farm animals and screeching monkeys, of tinkling chimes and hand-carved wooden water buffalo bells, of the tawdry and the breathtaking.

Sunday didn't know where to look first—at an artisan working her loom or at a rack of sterling silver chains, the links interwoven so closely that the necklace she picked up felt like liquid silver in her hand.

They moved on to the next booth. "These were originally used by Thai rice farmers," Simon explained as she examined the drawstring bags made of fabric and trimmed with cowrie shells.

At yet another table, Sunday studied a richly embroidered and beaded baseball cap. There was a sequined elephant on the front, and another on the bill. "This is wonderful," she exclaimed.

"It's called *Kalaga,*" Simon told her. "It's native to the remote northern hill country. The original tapestries were encrusted with rare gemstones and told stories of love, royalty and often elephants, a Thai symbol of luck."

She picked up a *Kalaga* tapestry vest from the same table. "The workmanship is extraordinary." Looking up at Simon, she said, "Could you ask this woman how many vests she can make in say—" she made an airy gesture with her hand "—a month?"

Simon spoke with the hill tribe woman for several minutes. Then he gave Sunday an answer of sorts. "The woman is called Ikat. Her entire village is involved in the production of the *Kalaga* vests and caps. She wishes to know how many you want."

Sunday smiled and nodded. "Please tell Ikat that I will return to discuss business with her."

The scenario was repeated several more times as they moved through the marketplace. Near the end of the bustling street, they came upon a display of silk cloth in bright, festive shades of pink, red and purple.

"Your trademark colors," Simon observed.

There were more bolts of material in green, brown and saffron. Sunday's head was swirling with images of what she could do with the fine Thai silk. "This is exactly what I've been looking for," she confided to him with barely suppressed excitement. "I'm going to create a whole collection around the things I've seen tonight." She clasped his arm. "Oh, Simon, this is everything I'd hoped it would be and more."

He brought his face closer. "It's only the beginning."

It was then that Sunday happened to look past him to where a young couple were browsing at a booth on the far side of the bazaar. She couldn't see their features clearly, but there was something vaguely familiar about the pair. For a moment, she even wondered if they could be the Grimwades. That wasn't possible, of course. The Australian couple had flown back to Bangkok two days ago.

Still . . .

Sunday was about to mention the incident to Simon, when she felt the first raindrop. Then another and another. Umbrellas seemed to magically appear from one end of the marketplace to the other. Within a minute or two, it began to rain in earnest.

"Let's find some shelter," Simon suggested, taking her by the elbow. "Here," he said, drawing her into the shadows of a nearby doorway.

"Does anybody live here?" she said, peering in the window of the small hut behind them.

"Nope. It's deserted," he said.

His eyes never left hers. His breath was fresh and sweet, yet masculine, with a hint of the strong coffee they'd drunk after dinner; it stirred the tendrils around her cheeks. His hands were on either side of her head as he backed her up against the wall of the primitive building.

"Simon." The voice didn't sound like hers.

"Sunday." His was different, somehow, as well. Husky. Guttural. Intense.

She could hear the *rat-a-tat-tat* of rain on the tin roof overhead. She could smell the scented blossoms on the wind, and the moisture in the air and the mountain dust. Over Simon's left shoulder, she could make out the glow of lantern light in the distance.

"We're a million miles from home," she murmured.

"More like eight or nine thousand, actually," he said, lowering his voice to a whisper.

He was making it impossible for her to keep her train of thought. "Maybe this isn't a good idea."

Simon moved his head. "Maybe it isn't."

She pushed at his chest; it was an ineffectual, half-hearted gesture at best. "Then why are we—?"

He eliminated the space between them. "Because we have to. I've known that since the afternoon Ho and his gang stopped us on the road to Lamphun." A heartbeat, then two. "So have you."

"Yes." The shadows closed around them. "I feel as if things are about to change."

"They are."

"Change can be frightening," she admitted.

"Change is inevitable."

Sunday tried to collect her wits. "I suppose you're right."

Simon looked down at her. "I know I'm right."

Held close to him as she was, she found his eyes unavoidable. "I don't look *up* to many men."

The corners of his beautiful mouth curved. "Literally or figuratively?"

Sunday swallowed. "Both."

Quick fingers closed on her wrist. Simon raised her hand to his mouth. Then he brushed his lips back and forth across the sensitive skin at the base of her thumb. "I'm going to kiss you."

She sucked in her breath. "Isn't that what you're doing?"

His eyes darkened. "Are you going to kiss me?"

Was she? Her heart was racing. "Yes."

The last inch between them disappeared.

Kissing Simon Hazard was a paradox. He was exactly what she'd expected, and he was far more than she'd bargained for. He was only several inches taller than she, but he was broad-shouldered, solid, muscular. There were few men who made Sunday feel small, dainty, petite, protected, when she stood beside them. Simon, it turned out, was one of them.

Then there was the taste of him, the smell of him, the feel of him and her reaction to him. She had been merely curious in the beginning, she told herself. But curiosity soon led to something else, and that something else was passion.

What did she know of passion?

She had a passion for strawberry ice cream, for that twilight time between evening and full-blown night, for the colors pink, red and purple. She was passionate about music, about good food, about the spring of the year, about the poetry of Wordsworth, Shelley, Walt Whitman.

But what did she know of passion between a man and a woman?

Very little. Her experience with the opposite sex was limited to a few groping kisses, an awkward caress or two, a bungling young man on a hot summer night, hurried, embarrassed, self-conscious.

Simon's kiss, Simon's caress—resolute, manly, impassioned—was a world away from that other time, that other place. His mouth was all that a man's mouth should be. His lips were soft, without being weak or insipid. His taste was intoxicating, slightly mysterious, definitely addictive. His touch was confident without being cocky. He wasn't sure of her; he was simply sure of himself, of how he felt, of what he wanted.

And it was abundantly clear from the way he kissed her, the way he caressed her, the way he used his body to gently pin her against the wall that what Simon Hazard wanted was her!

* * *

He'd made a mistake.

A big mistake.

A *huge* mistake.

He'd known for nearly three days that he was going to kiss Sunday Harrington. The anticipation had been growing inside him since the encounter with the bandits on the road to Lamphun.

He was no fool, Simon reminded himself. He knew sexual excitement and the threat of physical violence were sometimes flip sides of the same coin. It was one reason he hadn't acted on the impulse to kiss Sunday until now. He'd wanted to make sure that he knew what he was doing, that he was in control of the situation, that things didn't get out of hand.

Things were out of hand.

They'd made a mad dash to take cover from the rain. He'd bent toward Sunday to say something, promptly forgotten whatever it was he'd intended to say, and the next thing he knew, he was kissing her. Not once. Not twice. But again and again until both of them were breathing heavily, their lungs starved for oxygen, their hearts pounding.

It was crazy.

"This is crazy," he muttered against her mouth.

Sunday's arms snaked their way around his waist. "Crazy," she echoed.

"Insane," he added as he nuzzled her neck.

"Insane," she agreed.

"We're not a couple of kids." Simon took her face in his hands. "We're two mature and consenting adults."

Sunday mumbled something unintelligible.

"I've never done anything like this before," he confessed, catching her by the shoulders and giving her a tiny shake.

"Neither have I."

"As a grown man, I mean," he revised, stumbling over his own words, his own thoughts.

Simon slipped his hands down her arms and across her rib cage, then he covered her breasts. There was an immediate reaction from both of them. Her nipples protruded into his palms, grazing his skin, teasing and tickling him, making his hands itch to do so much more than caress her through the material of her dress and bra.

His own body reacted, as well. He could feel his flesh pressing against the zipper of his jeans, hard and rigid. About to explode, he was on the verge of embarrassing himself.

There was a sharp intake of air. At first, Simon thought it was his own. Then he realized it was Sunday's. She knew. How could she not know? His hips were grinding against hers.

"I was wrong," he growled, putting breathing room between them.

"About what?"

"My self-control." Hell, he was acting like someone half his age. "This was a mistake."

She reached up and traced the hard line of his jaw. "Don't say that."

"Why not?"

He felt her pause for a fraction of a second before she said, "Because I liked it."

"Liked it?"

"I loved it," she admitted in a husky voice.

It wasn't meant to be seductive. It wasn't meant to be a come-on. The woman didn't have a flirtatious bone in her body.

"You shouldn't say that to me, Sunday," he warned her.

She held herself very still. Huge green eyes stared at him warily. "Why not?"

Simon almost blurted out the truth: because he wanted to take her in his arms again, because he wanted to strip every last article of clothing from their bodies and stretch out on the soft, wet grass and make love all night long. Because he wanted, needed, to scratch this erotic itch. Because he wanted to bury himself so deeply inside her that neither of them would know where he ended and she began.

"Because I want you," he said through gritted teeth.

She frowned. "Want me?"

He swore softly, and after a slight hesitation said, "I want to make love to you."

Her mouth formed an O. "I—I'm sorry, Simon," she stammered. "I wasn't thinking. I didn't understand."

Who did think at a time like this? Who could? The brain shut down and instinct took over.

"I know I must seem very naive to you," Sunday began, concentrating on his chin.

She did.

Absentmindedly, she reached out and buttoned his shirt where it had come undone. "I haven't had a great deal of experience at this kind of thing."

He'd guessed as much.

"As a matter of fact," she said frankly, "I've lived pretty much like a . . ."

"Nun?" he supplied.

Simon didn't actually hear Sunday say yes, but he sensed it.

"If it's any comfort to you," he said, tucking a strand of red hair behind her ear, "I've been living for some time as a—"

"Monk?"

"Yeah. I guess that explains it," he proposed, with a crooked smile.

She stared at him, unblinking. "Explains what?"

"Our reaction—or maybe I should say our *over*-reaction—to each other."

She heaved a sigh. "It was a little intense."

"It quickly got out of control."

"We'll know better next time," she said.

If they were smart, if *he* was smart, there wouldn't be a next time.

Simon looked at the star-studded sky and held out his hand, palm up. "It's stopped raining."

Sunday stepped from the doorway of the hut. "Yes. It has."

"Perhaps we should go back to the night bazaar and see to your business," he suggested.

"Perhaps we should," she agreed, patting her hair and smoothing the front of her red dress.

Simon knew he had to do something, say something to relieve the tension between them. "I was right about one thing," he said as they made their way around the mud puddles that had appeared in the street.

"What's that?"

He slipped an arm around Sunday's shoulders and flashed her a devilish grin. "You're worth a hell of a lot more than three pigs."

Nine

"A map and a riddle, what do you think the man meant?" Sunday asked as she studied the piece of paper she had paid handsomely for by Thai standards. It was early the next morning, the sun was on the horizon and they were several hours into the arduous eight-hour drive from Chiang Mai to Mae Hong Son.

Simon kept his eyes on the tortuous mountain road. "I guess just that—it's a map and it's a riddle."

Sunday chewed on her lower lip and thought out loud. "I wonder what this symbol represents."

"Describe it to me," he suggested.

"It's a stylized circle with large scalloped edges. Inside the circle are four sets of lines that form four identical shapes. The shapes are similar to hearts. Oh, and each line ends in a fancy curlicue."

"A fancy curlicue?"

"How would you describe it?" she said, holding the map up just within his field of vision.

Simon took his eyes off the winding highway for a fraction of a second. "Hmong," he announced.

"Hmong?"

"Lisu, Hmong, Karen, Lahu, Muser, Akha—they're all hill tribes, each with its own language, its own customs, its own distinctive set of symbols. I won't say writing because some, like the Akha, have no written language."

"Tell me more about this Hmong symbol," she urged.

"It is called a *Pa Ndau,* which means a 'cloth flower,' and according to Hmong thinking, it attracts good spirits. But the design isn't a bunch of hearts. It's an elephant's footprint.

"The elephant being the symbol for luck and good fortune in this part of Asia," she said.

"You remembered."

"I remembered."

"The other symbol I caught a glimpse of is either Akha or Lisu. The geometric triangles are supposed to be the mountains that keep good spirits from fleeing."

"So we have an elephant footprint and a mountain range," she concluded.

"We have more than that," he reminded her. "There is the river Pai, as I mentioned that first day outside the Temple of the Reclining Buddha. The mountains may very well correspond to the mountains on a regular map, and the local tribespeople can tell you where the traditional elephant trails are.''

Sunday tried to be realistic, but her heart gave a leap. ''You mean, we might actually be able to pinpoint the location of the Hidden Buddha?''

''Within ten or fifteen kilometers,'' he cautioned. ''Assuming the map isn't a fake and assuming the Hidden Buddha is sitting right out in the open.''

''Oh.'' Sunday couldn't keep the disappointment out of her voice.

''Surely you knew it was a long shot.''

''Of course I knew it was a long shot.''

So much in life was a long shot, Sunday reflected as she turned her head and gazed out the side window of the Range Rover. Her career as a fashion model. Her success as a designer. Even this trip to Thailand. Most people never attempted in a lifetime half of what she had accomplished by the age of thirty.

Still, something was missing.

For years, she'd told herself that it was something she didn't want, didn't miss—at least not very often—and didn't need. Now she wasn't so certain.

Passion. Commitment. Desire. Dedication. Determination. She had taken the full gamut of her emotions and poured them into her career, her pursuit of an education, her business. There had been very little—if anything—left over to give to a personal relationship.

Men. They came in all shapes and sizes, some with intelligence and some without. Some men were kind, sensitive, artistic. Some were overloaded with testosterone and a competitive spirit. Some were workaholics. Some were out to build a name for themselves. Some thought they were God's gift to women. What she had never found, Sunday realized, was a man, *the* man, of her dreams.

What kind of man would he be?

A man of integrity. A man of honor and intelligence and common sense. He would be mature, self-reliant, self-confident—without being egotistical, of course. He would be successful. He would possess a keen wit and a flair for stimulating conversation.

The man of her dreams would be monogamous. He would love her, desire her, adore her, even worship the ground upon which she walked. He would excite her, make her heart beat faster, send sensual chills down her spine with his kiss, his caress.

Did such a man exist? Was there a Mr. Right somewhere for her? Or was she too much of an idealist? Too much of a romantic at heart? Had she set her sights too high? Could she, would she, ever find a man, *the* man for her?

"Improbable, but not impossible," stated Simon.

Sunday gave her head a shake; she had lost all track of time. "I beg your pardon."

"I said, it's improbable but not impossible."

She sat up a little straighter and stretched her legs out in front of her. "What is?"

"Finding the Hidden Buddha of the Heavenly Mist, of course."

"You were talking about the Buddha?"

An expression of puzzlement crossed his face. "What were you talking about?"

"The Buddha, of course," she said lightly as she opened her handbag and took out her sunglasses.

Sunday wasn't telling him the truth.

He'd been around enough wheeler-dealers and high-powered CEOs in his time to know when someone was lying. Of course, she was entitled to her privacy. She didn't have to share her every thought with him.

It was just that after last night, Simon admitted to himself, he was a little skittish. He only hoped he hadn't scared her off.

Sunday had claimed that she liked his kisses, his caresses. *Loved* them, in fact. But she wouldn't be the first woman to get cold feet in the harsh light of day.

Last night had been a sensory overload of exotic sights and sounds. A man and a woman, already attracted to each other, thousands of miles from home, found themselves alone in the shadows and the warm, tropical rain. Ending up in each other's arms hadn't exactly been a long shot.

So much in life was a long shot, though, Simon mused as he shifted gears and steered the Range Rover around the next bend in the road. His career in the navy. His success as a businessman. Making his first million before he was thirty. Hell, most people never attempted in a lifetime half of what he had already accomplished.

Still, something was missing.

For a long time, he'd had himself convinced that it was something he didn't want, didn't miss and didn't need. Now he wasn't so sure.

Passion. Commitment. Desire. Dedication. Determination. He had taken the full range of his emotions and poured them into his business career. There had been blessed little left to give to a personal relationship, but the occasional woman in his life had always understood and accepted that. She'd had no choice.

Women. They came in all shapes and sizes, some with intelligence and some without. Some were beautiful on the outside and some on the inside. Some were greedy, the kind who would do anything for fame and fortune. Some wanted a career. Some thought they were God's gift to men. What he had never found, Simon realized, was a woman, *the* woman, of his dreams.

What kind of woman would she be?

A woman with integrity. A woman with honor. Someone with a keen intelligence, a generous heart and plenty of old-fashioned common sense. She would be mature and self-confident, but not egotistical. A sense of humor was a must, as well as a positive attitude about life.

The woman of his dreams would love him and only him. She would be his wife, his best friend, his lover. She would excite him, make his heart pound like a brass drum, send chills down his spine with her kiss, her caress.

Did such a woman even exist? Was there a Ms. Right for him? Or was he too demanding? Had he set his sights too high? Could he, would he, ever find a woman, *the* woman for him?

"I suppose it's not impossible," Sunday ventured, interrupting his musings.

Simon frowned. "What's not impossible?"

"Finding the Hidden Buddha, of course."

"Stranger things have happened," Simon allowed. He picked up the thread of their conversation and carried on, "In this part of the world, archaeologists always seem to be stumbling upon the ruins of a city buried under centuries of neglect, or an ancient temple overgrown with trees and vegetation."

"Lost to time, even to memory," she murmured.

"Shrouded in mist and usually inaccessible."

She looked at him wonderingly. "Tell me about the City of Mist."

He could explain it in a word. "Unspoiled."

"Go on," Sunday said, encouraging him with her obvious interest in the subject.

"Mae Hong Son was literally cut off from the outside world for centuries. The first road leading in or out of the valley was built during the Second World War. It wasn't paved until 1968."

"Tell me more," she urged, turning toward him and tucking one leg under her.

"Two hundred years ago, Burmese settlers came across the border and settled in the valley. They built twin temples—Wat Chong Kham and Wat Chong Klang—and filled them with artifacts, religious treasures and rare pigeon's blood rubies." He hadn't thought of it before, but Sunday's hair was the color of the precious red stone. "The settlers called rubies *ma naw ma ya,* 'desire-fulfilling stones.'"

"I know that a large gem-quality ruby is thirty to fifty times more rare than a diamond, and much more expensive."

He gave a decisive nod of his head. "Which probably explains why a virtuous woman's price 'is far above rubies.'"

"And why wisdom 'is more precious than rubies,'" Sunday contributed.

Simon kept his eyes on the road as they talked. "Some years later, in 1831, a training camp for elephants was established in the valley, and a third temple was built on Mae Hong Son's highest hill. This temple housed a white marble Buddha."

"You make it sound...magical," she said.

"It is magical. And spectacular. And unlike any other place on earth," Simon said, and he meant it.

"'Nobody told me that I should see temples on high places,'" she quoted.

He crooked an eyebrow in her direction.

"Horace Walpole. 1772," she said. "According to Colonel Bantry, Walpole also said, 'I have seen gigantic places before but never a sublime one.'" She smiled. "Perhaps today you'll show me a sublime place."

It was some hours later that Simon turned off the narrow road, brought the Rover to a complete stop, stretched his arms over his head and told Sunday, "We're there."

She reached up and slowly removed her sunglasses. "Where?"

Simon could hear the bewilderment in her voice. He tried to see the rugged mountain terrain, the steep forty-five degree slopes and the dense forests from her point of view. "I guess it does look like the middle of nowhere."

Sunday laughed as she tucked her dark glasses back into her handbag. "It *is* the middle of nowhere."

He hoped she was a good sport. "We're going to enter the City of Mist the way everyone should."

"How's that?"

"On foot."

He'd obviously caught her by surprise. It was written all over her lovely face. "We're walking?"

"We're walking."

"What about the Rover?"

Simon grabbed his knapsack from the seat behind him. "We'll come back for it later."

"And our belongings?"

"Take only the necessities with you. The rest will be safe enough left in the vehicle. If there are any people around—"

"You're joking, of course," she interjected.

He had to admit they were the only human beings in sight. "If there are any people around, they won't disturb our stuff." He got out and locked the doors. "Follow me."

Sunday followed him.

"By the way," Simon said over his shoulder as an afterthought, "you aren't afraid of heights, are you?"

"No." There was a pause. "Why?"

"We cross here."

Sunday came up behind him. "Here?"

"Here," he said, pointing to the rope suspension bridge that began a few feet in front of them and ended in a shroud of white mist.

Ten

Sunday balked. "You expect me to walk across *that?*"

Simon turned and looked at her. "I thought you said you weren't afraid of heights."

"I'm not." She let a moment pass. "Usually."

They were standing on the edge of what she assumed was either a precipice or a great gorge or some kind of canyon. It was difficult to tell since a thick, white mist—perhaps it was a layer of low-level clouds—hung over the entire landscape.

She could make out dark shapes and shadows on the opposite side. Hills. Trees. A forest. From far below came the sound of rushing water, not that of a babbling brook or a meandering stream, but of a fast-running river.

Directly in front of them was a bridge.

The sides of the bridge were open, the handholds were woven of thick rope, and the floor, barely wide enough for two people to walk abreast, was constructed of narrow wooden slats. The suspension bridge stretched from their side of the ghostly precipice to the opposite bank. The other sound she could hear, Sunday suddenly realized, was the stridulation of cords and cables swaying in the wind.

"My God," she exclaimed. "It looks like something out of an Indiana Jones movie."

"Yes, it does," Simon agreed spiritedly.

"What's the name of the river below?"

"That is the river Pai."

"Then the bridge is—"

"Yup, it's the bridge on the river Pai."

Sunday groaned. "How can you make a joke at a time like this?"

There was a flash of teeth. "'He who laughs at himself never runs out of things to laugh at.'"

Sunday emitted a nervous laugh of her own, leaned forward from the waist and peered anxiously over the edge of the embankment. "How far down is it?"

Simon's answer seemed deliberately obtuse to her. "Far enough."

"I can't see the other side," she observed.

He made a production of staring into the mist. "I'm sure it's there. If it will make you feel any better, I'll go first," he volunteered.

With a flourish of her hand, she said, "Be my guest."

Simon walked onto the suspension bridge. "The key to a successful crossing is developing a rhythm to your gait."

"A rhythm to my gait," Sunday echoed, stepping onto the wooden platform after him. With the addition of their weight, the bridge began to sway from side to side. She sucked in her breath. "I wish it wouldn't do that. It makes me dizzy."

"Don't look down," he recommended.

"I'm not. I can't see anything, anyway," she grumbled.

"Keep your eyes on me" came the clipped instructions.

An irreverent question popped into Sunday's head, but she didn't voice it aloud. On exactly which part of him should she keep her eyes?

"You're unflappable, remember?" Simon said, obviously attempting to buoy her confidence.

She wiped her palms on her blue jeans. "Unflappable."

"No guts, no glory."

"No guts, no glory. No guts, no glory. No guts, no glory," she repeated like a mantra.

"How are you doing?"

"How do you think I'm doing?" she told him feelingly.

Her heart was lodged in her throat. Her hands were damp. Her stomach was doing acrobatics. Her legs were made of wobbly gelatin. She couldn't swallow. She couldn't breathe. She couldn't think.

"Life is an adventure," Simon called out to her. "Grab hold of it with both hands. Go for the gusto."

"Good grief, a pep talk," Sunday muttered under her breath as she inched her way along.

Simon halted, his feet planted solidly on the evenly spaced planks of the suspension bridge, then turned halfway around, swiveling from the hips, and held out his hand to her. "Trust me, Sunday. If you dare to take a chance, you will be rewarded beyond your wildest dreams." Then he smiled at her and the fear that had plagued Sunday only moments before seemed to magically disappear.

It was the darnedest thing.

"Take my hand," he urged.

She took a step toward him and placed her hand in his. He was warm and solid, trustworthy and sure. He made her feel safe in a world that was often far from it.

By the time they reached the opposite side, the sun had come out and the mist was quickly being burned off the hills. They stood on the summit and gazed back at the landscape: steep mountains, green forests, blue skies, a lingering cloud or two, the river Pai below.

"I have something I want to show you," Simon finally said in a secretive manner.

They hiked down the incline, through a thicket of native trees, across a rocky creek bed and up the next hill. They stopped. There, stretched out before them, lush and green and gently undulating, was a high mountain meadow.

"There is very little flat land in this region."

Sunday felt a vague sense of disappointment. The scenery was lovely, but somehow she'd expected more. "This is what you wanted to show me?"

"Not exactly," Simon answered as he prodded her closer to the field. "I want to show you a farm."

"A farm?" She was from Ohio; she had seen plenty of farms.

"This is a very special kind of farm. It's unlike any you have ever seen. I promise."

The meadow grass reached their knees; in some places, it was even hip high. Sunday looked closer. There were bits of color here, there, everywhere, in every shade of the rainbow.

She frowned. "Flowers?"

"There are flowers and vegetation of nearly all varieties that will grow at this altitude," Simon explained. "But what I wanted to show you was—"

They moved closer, and several of the specks of color rose in front of them and fluttered away.

Sunday held out her hand and said in a hushed tone, "Butterflies."

"Butterflies," Simon confirmed.

"Hundreds of them."

"Thousands."

A breeze came up, and suddenly the butterflies were airborne, thousands upon thousands of fluttering wings in gray and brown, scarlet, coral red and pink, azure, shades of purple and lavender, canary yellow and jade. Some were as small as her smallest fingernail; some were as large as her palm.

Sunday felt like laughing and crying at the same time. Her eyes brimmed with tears. Her throat constricted. The field of butterflies was unlike anything she had ever beheld. For several minutes, she didn't speak, couldn't speak.

"Now I have seen a sublime place," she finally said, turning to Simon. "You were right."

"Of course, I was right," he claimed with a satisfied grin. Then he grew serious. "I made you a promise. I always keep my promises."

Their eyes met. They took a step toward each other. Simon reached for her. She reached for him. And there, in that magical place, that sublime place, they kissed again.

This time he didn't taste of strong coffee and dark rain, Sunday noted in the recesses of her mind, but of sunshine and meadow grass. Yet this kiss was just as seductive, just as addictive, just as heart-stopping as last night's.

Simon took her breath away. At first, she was acutely aware that they were standing in a field of butterflies on the top of a mountain in Thailand. Then she promptly forgot where she was, who she was, why she was here. The world began and the world ended within the circle of Simon's arms.

It was the sound of childrens' laughter—high-pitched like the trill of songbirds, delighted and delightful, musical, carefree—that finally drove them apart.

Then the chant began: "*Sawat-dii,* Simon! *Sawatt-dii,* Simon!" Greetings, Simon!

"Don't tell me," Sunday speculated with a bemused smile. "You've been here before."

They were surrounded by a dozen children of all ages, faces smiling, a few behind shy giggles, arms raised, dressed in brightly colored hats and vests, pantaloons and woven jackets.

"In my wanderings I stopped and lived with this hill tribe for a few months," Simon offered as an explanation as they were carried along on a human tide toward the thatch-roofed village.

Sunday watched as he spoke to the children in their own dialect, as they responded to him, chatting with him animatedly, vying for his attention, eagerly seeking to be the one honored to walk beside him, to lead the way.

The village itself was a smattering of bamboo huts built on stilts. There was a single dirt street down the middle of the primitive town, not by design, but as a result of innumerable feet wearing away the grass and the underbrush. There were soybean fields beyond the village, and forests beyond the fields. An old man and woman were sitting side by side on the porch of their house, a smoking brazier in front of them. The scent of cooking hung heavy in the air.

Simon gave a respectful nod of his head as they passed, and Sunday followed suit. After all, this was Simon's place and Simon's people, in essence. She was merely a visitor.

They came to a second bamboo hut. A man slightly older than Simon emerged, and they greeted each other like long-lost brothers, clasping each other by the hand and shoulder in a ritual embrace, speaking in excited voices, gesturing toward the meadow she and Simon had just traversed.

Simon motioned to her. Sunday stepped forward to stand beside him. "This is the headman of our village," he told her. "His name is Tget." A woman came out of the hut and joined them. "This is Tget's wife. Her name is Siri."

Siri gave a polite bow, smiled and spoke one of the few English words she knew. "Wel-come." Then she beckoned with her hand. *"Maa."* Come.

Simon slipped off his dusty cowboy boots. Sunday untied her walking shoes. They were left behind at the bottom of the porch steps. She knew it was considered good manners to remove any footwear before entering someone's home or a temple.

The four of them sat cross-legged on a woven floor mat. Simon and Tget spoke of recent events in the village. Siri offered them water, a courtesy in Thai and hill-tribe cultures. Occasionally, Simon translated part of the conversation for her.

Later, they shared a meal of rice, cooked beans and some kind of baked root that tasted a little like a sweet yam. Tget and Siri escorted them to the front porch where they sat and watched the sunset together. Music and singing followed to celebrate Simon's homecoming. Then the fires were allowed to burn low in the braziers, exhausted children were put to bed and families retired for the night.

Tget spoke again, and Simon turned to her. "The village has invited us to stay. My old house has been made ready. Would you like to spend the night in Houi Sia Tao?"

"It's a great honor to be asked, isn't it?"

"It's a great honor to be asked," Simon confirmed.

"I would love to stay," she replied.

He replaced his cowboy boots, and Sunday, her shoes, and then the four of them walked through the village to what had been Simon's home for a few months. There were fresh wildflowers tied to the front of the bamboo door and fragrant grass mats covering the porch floor. Inside was a small, low table, a lighted brass oil lamp, pillows to sit on, a carved chest, two sleeping mats and a stack of neatly folded blankets.

Simon's voice was modulated. "I have thanked Tget and Siri for this honored house, for preparing our welcome, for the fresh wildflowers, for the baskets of fruit and bread, for the polite offer of water and the special rice cakes."

Sunday bowed discreetly and said to the hill-tribe man and woman, "Thank you very much. You have been most kind to this *farang*."

"We will remove our shoes again before entering the house," Simon told her, and they did.

Then Tget began to speak.

As he spoke, he took a strand of smooth stone beads from around his neck—the beads were the colors of the rainbow, the colors of the butterflies in the field— and recited what sounded to Sunday like some kind of blessing.

Simon held out his hand. Sunday looked into his eyes, and then placed her hand in his. Tget wrapped the strand of beads around their wrists. The man took an earthenware jug from Siri and poured a small amount of cool, clear water over their joined hands. Then he began to chant.

A shiver coursed along Sunday's spine. Intuitively, she knew this was a special hill-tribe ceremony between a man and a woman.

It was Simon's tone of voice—calm, almost nonchalant, yet somehow fraught with meaning—that lifted her face. "Tget is asking if you are my woman."

Sunday did not find the question as preposterous now as she would have at their first meeting in the Celestial Palace. She and Simon had shared so much in the intervening days.

Could it really be less than two weeks since they'd strolled through the gardens outside the Temple of the Reclining Buddha? It seemed so long ago, a lifetime ago.

In an odd way, she'd shared more of herself with Simon Hazard than with any other man of her acquaintance. Certainly no one had seen her day after day in the same jeans and sweater, sans shower, sans makeup, sans hairstyle.

Was she Simon's woman?

No.

Would she like to be his woman?

Sunday recalled his kisses, his caresses last night in the rain. She thought of his kiss this afternoon as they stood in a field of butterflies. There was something about this place and these people. She couldn't have lied if she'd wanted to.

Sunday nodded her head and, not without a certain amount of trepidation answered, "Yes, I am his woman."

The question must have been repeated for Simon, for she heard him reply in his husky baritone, first in the hill-tribe dialect and then in English, "Yes, I am her man."

Tget concluded his chant. He reached up and touched his hand first to her cheek and then to Simon's, making some kind of mark with another drop or two of cool water. Then he and Siri smiled upon them, said something in their own language, gave a slight bow, backed out of the hut and retreated into the night.

It was several minutes before either of them spoke.

Simon broke the silence. "Thank you," he said.

She looked up at him in the flickering lamplight. "For what?"

"For graciously accepting the village's invitation to stay here, for treating these people with kindness and respect, for going along with the ceremony and for not rejecting me in front of Tget and his people," he said, unraveling the necklace of stone beads and placing it carefully on the small table.

"I did all of those things because I wanted to," she informed him.

"I know," Simon said, dropping his eyes to the floor mat. "But you may not have understood the significance of everything we just did." He looked up and gave her a tentative smile. "The good news is that nothing is binding outside tribal territory."

She folded her arms under her breasts. "Perhaps you should tell me exactly what the ceremony was with the beads and the water."

"Now, Sunday, I want you to keep a couple of things in mind," Simon began as if he were addressing a business meeting.

It was not an auspicious beginning, in her opinion. She was instantly on her guard. "Yes?"

Simon gnawed on his bottom lip and then wiped the back of his hand across his mouth. "First, as I mentioned, it isn't binding."

Her eyebrows rose a fraction of an inch. "Go on."

"Second, I did it for your own good."

Her eyebrows went up another notch. "For *my* good?"

He nodded. "These are simple, unsophisticated people. In their view, there are only two kinds of women."

"And, pray tell, what are those?"

He dropped the bomb. "Wives and the type you find at—"

"The Celestial Palace?"

"Exactly."

Sunday swallowed. "I see."

"I'm glad that you do," Simon said, visibly relieved. That seemed to settle the matter as far as he was concerned. He studied the layout of the hut. "Which bed do you prefer?"

"Whoa!"

His head snapped around. "Was there something else?"

She tapped her cotton-socked foot on the bamboo floor. "Just one or two points I'd like clarified."

"Fire away."

She was tempted, Sunday admitted to herself. "About the water and the beads and the chanting," she prompted.

Simon appeared vaguely uneasy, perhaps even a little uncomfortable. "It was a kind of..." He seemed determined to find the right words. "...betrothal ceremony."

She looked up sharply. "You mean like engaged to be engaged."

He stuffed his hands into the front pockets of his jeans. "Not exactly."

"Then *exactly* what was it?"

He took another stab at an explanation. "It was more like an old-fashioned betrothal."

Sunday was starting to get an odd feeling in the pit of her stomach. "Historically, a betrothal was a promise to marry."

Simon rocked back and forth on the heels of his bootless feet. "Yup, it was."

"It was legally and morally binding in the eyes of society, in the eyes of the church, in a court of law."

"Yup."

"It often meant the couple engaged in..." she searched for a delicate way to put it "...full marital relations."

Simon permitted himself a small sigh. "Yup."

"These people think we're married, or the next thing to it, don't they?"

Simon jerked his hands out of his pockets and then seemed to realize he didn't know what to do with them. He settled on hooking his thumbs through his belt loops. "That's about the size of it."

Sunday kept her eyes straight ahead and level with his chest. She had no intentions of finding out about the size of anything, under the circumstances.

"I'll take the bed on the right," she announced.

Eleven

She was in love with Simon.

It hit Sunday like a ton of bricks as she stripped down to her bra and panties and slipped beneath the blankets spread out on her sleeping mat.

"Simon, you can come back inside now," she called to him, hoping that he wouldn't notice the heightened emotion in her voice, or, if he did, that he would chalk it up to the extenuating circumstances in which they found themselves.

In the eyes of these hill-tribe people, she and Simon were married, or the next thing to it.

Simon opened the door and reentered the single-room bamboo hut. Sunday could see his features clearly in the lamplight: the high forehead, the dark eyebrows, the aristocratic nose, the full mouth, the

strong line of his jaw and chin. Somewhere in the back
of her mind, it registered that he must have shaved this
morning before leaving their hotel in Chiang Mai;
there were signs of a five o'clock shadow on his face
but not an actual beard.

She wondered if all of the Hazard men were as rug-
gedly handsome as this one.

Simon unbuttoned his denim shirt, yanked his arms
out of the sleeves and hung the shirt up on a rusty nail
that was pounded into the back of the door.

Sunday couldn't take her eyes off him as he un-
dressed. He was all bronzed skin and bronzed muscles, with a smattering of black hair in the center of his
chest. The hair narrowed to a thin arrow over his taut
abdomen and then eventually disappeared beneath the
belt line of his blue jeans.

At some point, she realized that Simon was deliberately *not* looking at her. He avoided her eyes all the
while he removed his shirt and even when he leaned
over to extinguish the oil lamp.

The hut was plunged into darkness. The next sound
was the distinctive rasp of a zipper being undone; he
was taking off his jeans. Then she heard, rather than
saw, Simon stretch out on the sleeping mat a few feet
from her own.

Sunday didn't move a muscle. She simply lay there
in the dark with her arms straight down at her sides
and the covers pulled up to her chin. Her eyes gradually adjusted to the sparse amount of light that fil-
tered into the room through the bamboo slats. She
turned her head and stared at the shadowy outline she

knew was Simon's profile. She sensed somehow that his eyes were wide open.

It couldn't be love.

Simon couldn't be the man of her dreams. He didn't come close to fitting the description.

Infatuation—that's what it was. She was infatuated with him because he was different from the men she usually met, the type who were impeccably groomed, impeccably dressed and impeccably mannered. It was odd, Sunday reflected as she lay beneath the handwoven blankets, but there was a softness to the men she knew. She hadn't been aware of it before, but it was perfectly obvious to her now.

Simon, on the other hand, was hard. Rock-hard. Perhaps *strong* was the better word. It wasn't a skin-deep kind of strength, either. It was the kind of strength that went all the way through the man, all the way into his heart and soul and mind, from the tips of his scuffed cowboy boots to the top of his unruly head of hair.

Nonsense! Simon Hazard was just a man like any other man. "Who are you trying to kid?"

It wasn't until a masculine voice said, "Who are you trying to kid about what?" that Sunday realized she had spoken out loud.

She didn't answer the question. Instead, she made apologies. "I'm sorry. I hope I didn't wake you up."

"You didn't. I wasn't asleep." Simon also wasn't about to be deterred. "Who are you trying to kid?"

"It was nothing. I was simply thinking out loud," Sunday said.

She tried to swallow the lump in her throat and failed. She consoled herself with the thought that it wasn't every day a woman had to face the fact she'd fallen in love with a man who was a cowboy, a ne'er-do-well, an adventurer, not to mention a tour guide!

"You sleepy?" Simon asked.

"No." She was wide-awake. "Are you?"

"Nope."

"Do you want to—" she tried to swallow the strange lump again "—talk?"

"Talk?" She could hear the amusement in his voice. "Sure. Why not? What should we talk about?"

Love. Sex. Marriage. Children.

How did he feel about commitment? How did he feel about her? Was the attraction between them merely physical or did he think it went deeper?

She picked a safer topic. "Are you planning to stay in Thailand?"

"I don't know."

Silence.

"What kind of job did you have back in the States?"

"I was a businessman."

It wasn't much of an answer. Then it hit her. Good grief, maybe Simon didn't want to talk about the past, maybe he'd been involved in something shady, or something secretive, or something he wouldn't—or couldn't—talk about.

Sunday wasn't entirely sure where to go from here. But the problem was solved for her.

"Do you mind if I ask you a question?" Simon said.

She adjusted the small pillow under her head. "No." At least she didn't think so.

"Have you ever been married?"

"No." She hesitated only a fraction of a second. "Have you?"

"Nope." There was a rustling noise. Simon had turned onto his side. He was facing her now. She could discern the outline of his chest, his hips, his long legs. He had his head propped up on one arm; the other arm was extended out in front of him. "Now that we've told Tget and Siri that you're my woman and I'm your man, it feels different somehow, doesn't it?" he observed.

"Yes."

"I didn't expect that," he confessed.

"Neither did I."

"I mean, we both know the ceremony was strictly a formality."

"Strictly a formality," she echoed.

"It isn't binding in any way, shape or form, according to our legal and social system."

"True."

"Then why do I feel different?"

"I don't know." Her mouth was dry. "But so do I."

Suddenly, out of the blue, Simon announced, "What I feel, Sunday, is married."

So did she. It was the craziest thing.

He continued. "Frankly, with my family history, I've always thought of marriage as something you put on and took off at will . . . kind of like a suit coat."

No doubt his father's cavalier attitude toward marriage was to blame for that.

"It was Grand Central Station around our house," Simon went on. "A constant parade of ex-wives, stepchildren, half brothers, new spouses, old spouses and an assortment of relatives that, as a kid, I never could figure out how I was related to."

Poor Simon.

"At least my parents were married for most of my childhood," he told her. "Since then, Dad has decided to change his *mistress* every two or three years, rather than his *wife.*"

Sunday was mildly shocked. "How old is your father?"

"A robust and amazing eighty-five, which makes him old enough to be my grandfather."

"People have children at all stages of life," she said weakly.

She could see Simon's chest rise and fall with each lungful of air he took. "I don't think anyone should have children at the age my father was when I was born."

Sunday did some quick arithmetic. "Fifty, more or less?"

"More. The difference in my parents' ages was one of their biggest problems. My mother was thirty years younger than my father when they were married. She wanted a child. He didn't. After all, by then he already had four sons and four ex-wives. Mom got her way...for a while." Simon paused. "How old are you?"

Sunday wasn't concerned with being coy about her age. "Thirty. How old are you?"

"Thirty-two." Simon absentmindedly rubbed his hand back and forth across his bare chest. "Tell me about your mother and father."

"My family is perfectly ordinary." She liked it that way.

"What is perfectly ordinary in—?"

"Cincinnati, Ohio."

She could almost imagine the raised masculine eyebrow as Simon repeated, "Cincinnati, Ohio?"

"My father is a dentist in Cincinnati."

"You have beautiful teeth."

"Thank you." She smiled to herself in the dark. "My mother is a high school English teacher. I have a younger brother who is studying to be an orthodontist. There are a few aunts and uncles on each side of the family tree, a number of cousins—several of whom we prefer not to claim—two sets of healthy grandparents and a great-grandmother who enjoys being a bit outrageous and a bit eccentric."

"Well, if you can't be a bit outrageous and a bit eccentric by the time you're a great-grandmother, when can you be?" Simon ventured.

"That's what Eleanor always says." She wondered if she was boring him with such trivial talk. Not that Simon gave any indication of being bored. In fact, he seemed inordinately interested in hearing about her family. "That's where I get my red hair—from Eleanor."

"Eleanor is your great-grandmother?"

Sunday nodded. "That's one of her eccentricities. When she turned ninety, she suddenly insisted that we all call her by her first name." She drew a deep breath and let it out slowly. "Unlike some of my relatives, at least Eleanor didn't blink an eyelash at the *Sports Illustrated* cover."

"I think I'd like to meet your great-grandmother," he said. Then he added, "Think you'll ever be a great-grandmother?"

"First, I'd have to become a mother and a grandmother, in that order." Sunday counted to three. "Since I'm thirty and unmarried, I would say the chances are fairly slim." In spite of the hill-tribe ceremony, they weren't married and they both knew it.

Simon cleared his throat. "Surely a beautiful woman like you must have had dozens of marriage proposals."

"A few."

"A few?"

"Fewer than you might think," she said, digging her teeth into her lower lip.

"Why didn't you accept any of them?"

"I had my reasons," she said, hedging.

Simon was like a bulldog with a tasty bone between his teeth. He wasn't about to give it up or to let it go. "Give me one good reason," he prodded.

"Well," Sunday began, trying to sort out her scattered thoughts, "I think all of us want to be loved for who we are, not for what we appear to be. Men—some men, anyway—are interested in having a fashion model draped over their arm like a decoration or a prize, like something they've won at the county fair."

"A successful man can feel the same way, that a woman is only interested in appearances...like how big his bank account appears to be." Simon returned to his original line of questioning. "Tell me another reason you haven't married."

She wasn't going to be the only one to bare her soul. "I think it's your turn."

"Okay." There was a faint abrasive sound of skin rubbing against skin. Simon was moving his hand back and forth across his chest again. "I guess I haven't found a woman I want to spend my entire life with."

"I haven't found a man I want to spend my entire life with," she stated.

"My turn again?"

"Yes."

"I've never met a woman who I thought could be my best friend, my lover, my wife and the mother of my children."

"And I've never met a man who I thought could be my best friend, my lover, my husband and the father of my children."

"No fair," he told her. "You can't keep repeating what I say. You have to give your own reasons."

"All right." Sunday pressed her lips together while she considered the wisdom—or foolhardiness—of telling Simon the truth. "I've never been crazy in love." Until now.

"Neither have I," he claimed.

"I've never been with a man who made me forget where I was, who I was, what I was doing." She had forgotten all of those things and more last night when Simon had kissed her in the rain.

"I may have lost my head once or twice when I was a kid," he volunteered, "but it's been so many years ago that I can't remember where or when." Then, in a husky baritone that sent shivers down her spine, he confessed, "I lost my head last night, Sunday."

"I lost my head, too, Simon."

"We're not a couple of kids."

"No, we aren't."

He hesitated. "I've been wondering what it means."

"So have I." But she had a pretty darn good idea.

"I'm not out to seduce you."

Sunday was momentarily taken aback. "And I'm not out to seduce you," she assured him.

"I'm not interested in collecting lovers like trophies," he added.

"Neither am I."

"I've been celibate for some time."

"Me, too." Longer than he could possibly imagine.

"I'm an adult. And an adult doesn't need to bed the first attractive member of the opposite sex he or she meets in order to satisfy any physical urges."

Sunday could feel her cheeks growing warm. "I'm an adult, as well," she said a little too loudly.

"I believe it's a matter of mind over body."

"It certainly is." Her mind was certainly on his body.

"Which makes it all the more puzzling," Simon said in a meaningful tone.

She was half-afraid to ask. "Makes *what* all the more puzzling?"

"You," he drawled.

"Me?"

"I can't stop thinking about you, Sunday. I can't stop dreaming about you. And I can't seem to keep my hands off you."

She groaned softly. "Simon—"

"If you tell me that you don't feel the same way, I'll back off immediately," he promised.

"I can't." She took in a tremulous breath and let it out again. "I do feel the same way."

"Are you sure?"

"I'm sure."

There was an anticipatory silence.

"Do you want me, Sunday?"

"Yes." She had to take a chance. "Do you want me, Simon?"

"Yes, dammit."

Sunday said rather rapidly, "At first, I assumed it was nothing more than a rush of adrenaline because armed bandits had stopped us on the road. Last night, I blamed it on the tropical rain, the fact that we were finally alone, the excitement of the marketplace, the exotic atmosphere. Then, this afternoon in the field—"

"You decided it had to be the butterflies, or the sublime feeling that comes from standing on top of the world?"

"Something like that."

"It could still be any or all of those things," he reminded her needlessly.

"I know," she said in a half whisper.

"We're a long way from home."

"Eight or nine thousand miles, I believe you estimated."

"There is a risk involved."

She wet her lips. "What was it you said to me this afternoon just before we crossed the bridge on the river Pai?"

She heard a heavy masculine sigh from Simon's side of the hut. "If you dare to take a chance, you will be rewarded beyond your wildest dreams." Then he spoke kindly, reasonably, measurably. "That's a pretty tall order, Sunday."

"No guts, no glory."

He laughed softly. "I know. I know. And nothing ventured, nothing gained."

She licked her lips again. "I wish—" She stopped herself before she completed the sentence.

"What do you wish?"

This time she said it. "I wish you would kiss me."

Simon froze. "Once I start, I won't want to stop," he warned her.

"Neither will I."

"If I kiss you, I'll want to touch you."

"I'll want to touch you, too."

"If I touch you, I can damn well guarantee I'm going to want to make love to you."

"That makes two of us."

There was silence for a heartbeat. Then he said, "Does it seem warm in here to you, or is it me?"

Sunday surprised herself by laughing out loud. "I think it's us."

Simon stood up and crossed to one of the windows. He pushed open the bamboo shade, and silvery moonlight poured into the hut. Sunday could see him clearly now. He was wearing only a pair of shorts. His body had obviously already reacted to their conversation and the promise of what was to come. She had caught just a glimpse of him, but a glimpse was enough.

Simon leaned his elbow on the primitive windowsill and inhaled the cool, clear night air. He exhaled slowly and turned his head. "I want you to understand that if you change your mind at any time, all you have to do is speak up and tell me."

"I will." But she wasn't going to change her mind. She wanted to make love with him and to him. She wanted it more than she'd ever wanted anything in her life.

"There's a first-aid kit in my knapsack, so you don't have to worry about the necessary precautions," he said.

They weren't irresponsible. They were going into this with their eyes open.

"Now, what was it you were wishing for?" he said in a voice filled with sensual promise as he walked toward her.

"I was wishing you would kiss me," she reiterated as he came down beside her on the sleeping mat.

For an instant, Sunday could see past him to the window; it encased the large, round moon like a picture frame. Then Simon bent over her and the moon was blocked from view. She could feel his breath on her face. She could see his features in the silvery light. Her heart was suddenly pounding in her ears. She wanted to kiss him, to taste him, to touch him. God, she wanted him.

"Just one thing," she said.

"Shoot."

"Are you certain it isn't the cover girl in the purple bikini you're interested in kissing?"

"I'm sure the cover girl was stunning, but it's the woman who intrigues me," Simon murmured as he brushed his lips across hers. "I'm not interested in the past, Sunday, only in the present, only in the here and now."

"The here and now. Yes, that's what I'm interested in, too." Not his past. Not who he'd been. Not what he'd been. Only who and what he was at this moment.

Simon kissed her and, dear God, it happened all over again. First, she seemed to have a heightened awareness of her surroundings: the play of moonlight and shadows on the walls of the bamboo hut, the breadth of his shoulders, the faint scent of the oil lamp on the table, of exotic incense, of fresh fruit and wildflowers. Then these things receded somewhere into the background and soon vanished altogether, and what was left . . . was Simon.

Simon with his smooth, demanding, cajoling, intoxicating mouth. Simon with his strong, nimble, caressing fingers. Simon with hands that knew exactly where to touch her and how to touch her. Simon with his hard, muscular, incredibly masculine body.

"Are we crazy?" she whispered against his lips.

"Yes," he declared, delving into her mouth with his tongue. "Crazy about each other."

"Is this infatuation?"

"Possibly," he allowed, trailing his lips along her bare shoulder, nudging aside the strap of her bra.

"Is it sex?"

"I certainly hope so," he muttered, nibbling on her ear.

"Is it love?"

Simon's head lifted, and Sunday could see the dark intensity in his eyes, the frown on his handsome features, the set of his jaw. She reached up and threaded her fingers through the slightly mussed curls at his nape. She ran her hands along the smooth muscles of his upper arms, his chest, his torso, his back.

"Is it love?" he pondered out loud.

"I shouldn't have asked," she quickly rescinded in a small voice.

"Why not?" he said. "I've asked myself the same thing."

The beating of her heart was a painful throb in her chest. The depth of her emotions made her voice quiver, her hands tremble, her pulse pound. "Do you have the answer?"

Simon shook his head from side to side. "I wish I did." He cupped her chin in his palm and gazed intently into her eyes. "I haven't had much experience with real, true love, the everlasting kind of love, Sunday."

"Neither have I."

"We'll have to wing it, then."

She found herself nodding her assent. "Play it by ear."

"Take it one step at a time." He touched his lips to her mouth, to her shoulder, to her earlobe. "Where were we?" He moved lower to her breast, pushing the soft material of her bra away. He located her nipple and flicked the tip of his tongue back and forth across the sensitive nub. "Were we here?" he muttered thickly.

"Yes," she said on a ragged sigh.

Very quickly, Sunday was a mindless, witless, speechless mass of sensitive nerve endings and thrilling sensations. She was aware of being caressed, of strong hands clasping her by the buttocks and lifting her hips off the sleeping mat. She knew the moment she was naked, and realized Simon was, too.

She felt as free as the winged butterflies in the field. She flew. She soared. She hovered, suspended in mid-air.

Touching Simon with a butterfly-light caress, she heard him groan and felt him shiver. She smiled with satisfaction when he told her how much she pleased him, how much she pleasured him.

She felt his hand on her, his fingers slipping in and out of her, and then the hard probing of his body, the demanding thrust of his hips. She took all of him in and he filled her. His name became a litany of desire, of need, of fulfillment.

It began slowly, gradually, in the center of her body, somewhere deep inside her, a kind of singing sensation, followed by ripples of pleasure that radiated down to the tips of her toes and up to the last hair on the top of her head, covering her with goose bumps, setting even her teeth on edge.

Then that elusive something Sunday was seeking overtook her, and she cried out his name one more time as she felt herself hurled into space. "Simon!"

* * *

"I think we're going to have to redefine sublime," Simon proposed when he felt like talking again.

Hell, who did he think he was kidding? When he was *able* to talk again.

Sunday made a soft, cooing sound in the back of her throat that came out, "Hmmm."

He went up on his elbows and took the brunt of his considerable weight off her. He was still inside her, still partially hard and getting harder again by the second. He'd never felt like this before. Sex had never felt like this. Simon corrected himself: making love had never been like this. It was a damn paradox. He was weaker than a kitten; he felt as if he could conquer whole worlds single-handedly. He was satiated, and yet he wanted Sunday again immediately.

It didn't make sense.

Maybe love didn't make sense.

On the one hand, he loved the sound of Sunday's voice, the scent of her skin, the surprisingly full breasts, the long legs that went on forever. On the other hand, what he loved about her had nothing to do with any of those things. It was her laughter, her natural sweetness, her kindness to people, her sense of humor.

He was thinking too much.

Sunday wiggled beneath him and a sharp sensation—God, it was pure physical pleasure—shot through Simon. He couldn't stop the groan that issued forth from his lips.

Sunday's eyes blinked open. "Are you all right?"

He moved a fraction of an inch first this way and then that way, reminding himself all the while to breathe. "That depends on what you mean by all right," he said through gritted teeth.

"Are you in pain?"

Beads of perspiration broke out on his forehead and upper lip. "Not exactly."

"Then what are you?" she inquired in a puzzled tone.

"Aroused," he replied bluntly.

Her mouth opened and closed on a soundless O. "I see," she said at last.

He wondered if she did. "Are you all right?"

"That depends on what you mean by all right," she said, smiling a Mona Lisa smile and rotating her hips against his.

Simon sucked in his breath. Sunday was playing with fire. So much as another twinge by either of them and he would go up in flames.

"Are you sleepy?" she asked, lightly raking her nails down his back until a shudder passed through him.

"No." Hell, he was wide-awake. "Are you?"

She shook her head. "I'm not the least bit sleepy."

He tried his best to hold still, but his pelvis began to thrust forward as if of its own volition. "Do you want to talk?"

"Talk?" Simon could hear the bemusement in Sunday's voice. "Is that what you call it? Well, I suppose it is a form of communication. Silent communication."

Enough talk.

Simon bent his head and covered Sunday's mouth with his. He could tell when he had her complete at-

tention, when every rational thought had fled her
mind; she moaned and wrapped her arms tightly
around his waist and her legs around his hips.

He began to move inside her. He gave in to the
temptation to nip at her ear, to delve into her mouth
with his tongue, to suckle her breast, all the while
driving his flesh deeper and deeper into the seductive
sweetness of hers.

The blood was pounding in Simon's veins. He felt
as if he were on a collision course with a runaway
freight train. He couldn't stop now even if he wanted
to... and he didn't. He'd simply have to hold on for
dear life and see it through to the end.

The moment was nearly upon him. He heard his
own approaching shout of triumph. Her name was on
his lips. It echoed in his head. "Sunday! Sunday!"

Those lovely inner female muscles tightened around
him, squeezed him, caressed him, and he went flying
over the edge.

It was much later—he had lost all track of time—
that Simon became aware of the moonlight and the
starlight flooding the room of the primitive hut.

He rolled onto his side and gathered Sunday in his
arms. A strand of her hair—it was like red silk—
caught on the stubble of his beard. He gently brushed
it away and nuzzled her neck for a moment. She
smelled of the night and lovemaking and wildflowers.

It was then and there that Simon made a vow. He
would give this woman whatever her heart desired: the
sun, the moon, the stars in the heavens. He would be-
stow upon her anything and everything it was in his
power to give.

What had the stranger said that first day in the garden outside the Temple of the Reclining Buddha?

"Only a few men see the world that can be theirs for the asking. You are one of these men, are you not?"

Then the small wiry man in the dark trousers and the white shirt had offered to sell him the precious piece of paper.

"What is it?"

"It is a riddle. It is a map."

"Where will this map lead me?"

"It will lead you to happiness and riches."

Simon stroked Sunday's hair. The slow, even rhythm of her breathing told him that she'd fallen asleep. His own eyes were growing heavy, but a last thought occurred to him as he drifted off.

Maybe the Thai gentleman had been right. Maybe on this journey to the north, he would find happiness and the kind of riches he knew money could never buy.

Twelve

"Are you sure this is the path that leads to happiness and riches?" Sunday muttered as she trudged along behind Simon. It looked suspiciously like another hike through the woods to her.

"Tget studied your map and then spoke to the elders of the village," Simon said, setting a brisk pace. "One of them seemed to remember hearing a childhood story about a hidden Buddha. Tget and I think it may be your Hidden Buddha of the Heavenly Mist."

"Sounds like a long shot to me," Sunday grumbled. "I'd rather be in bed," she said loud enough for him to hear.

Simon turned and glanced back over his shoulder at her. "In bed?"

"Sleeping."

"Don't kid yourself," he said with a husky laugh. "If we were still in bed, we wouldn't be sleeping."

He was right.

The last thing she remembered after they'd made love a second time the previous night was the sight of Simon's face, the sound of Simon's voice and Simon's arms wrapped securely around her. She had fallen asleep with his name on her lips and his indelible imprint on her heart, her body, her soul.

She had awakened at dawn to find him whistling happily, moving around the bamboo hut, then talking and laughing with the other villagers as they prepared for their day.

When he'd kissed her good-morning, she had seen the sensual hunger in his eyes, tasted it on his lips, and Sunday had known that sleeping was the last thing on both their minds.

"What about the riddle and the symbols?" she finally said, harkening back to what he'd told her on the drive from Chiang Mai several days before.

"The hill-tribe people don't have maps, as we know them, but one of the elders drew the mountains and the traditional elephant tracks in the dirt at my feet."

"I suppose you memorized all of it."

"Yes, I did." Simon walked on. "According to Buddhist legend, all elephants were once white and flew through the heavens. Indeed, it was a white elephant who one day entered the sleeping Queen's side. From this virgin birth, some five hundred years before Christ, was born Prince Siddhartha, who would later renounce all worldly possessions and become Lord Gautama Buddha.''

"No wonder the elephant is a revered symbol in this part of the world," Sunday said as they made their way through the forest.

"Don't forget," Simon called to her over his shoulder. "Walk exactly where I walk. We wouldn't want to accidentally disturb a nesting cobra."

"*Not* disturbing a nesting cobra is real high on my list of priorities," Sunday said, making sure she stepped where Simon stepped. Frankly, she didn't see any evidence of cobras or elephants. "Are you sure this is an ancient elephant trail?"

"Yup."

A half hour later, she asked, "Are you sure this is the *right* ancient elephant trail?"

"I'm sure."

Without a word of warning, Simon came to a halt directly in front of her. Sunday ran smack-dab into him; it was like hitting a brick wall. She opened her mouth to speak.

"Shh." He held a finger up to his lips.

She clamped her mouth shut.

Simon cocked his head to one side and listened intently. Then he silently backtracked, retracing his own steps some twenty or thirty paces along the trail. He stood motionless and stared at the forest behind them. Finally, he returned to where she waited.

"What was that all about?" she asked in a whisper.

"I thought I heard something," he said quietly.

"Something?" Cold sweat trickled down her back. "You mean like a wild animal?"

Dark eyes rested thoughtfully on her. "I thought I heard footsteps."

"Footsteps?"

"Human footsteps," Simon spelled out for her.

The man was making her nervous. "You're giving me goose bumps," she said candidly.

Simon flashed her a dazzling smile. "That's what a man always likes to hear."

"I didn't mean *those* kind of goose bumps," she quickly denied.

"Of course, you did. You're just too shy to admit it," he claimed, unsheathing the machete dangling from his belt.

Her eyes opened wide. "That's some weapon you've got there."

"Yes, it is."

She stared at him. "It's big."

He grunted.

"It's huge."

"Thank you," he said with a wicked grin.

Sunday could feel herself blush right down to her already red roots. She made a self-conscious gesture. "I meant your weapon...your sword...your blade...whatever you call that darn thing in your hand."

Simon seemed to be biting the corners of his mouth against another grin. "I know what you meant."

They continued on their way. The forest floor was thick with vegetation. The trees overhead formed a natural canopy. When the underbrush on either side of the historic elephant track encroached too closely, Simon cleared a path in front of them, swinging his machete from side to side.

"I haven't seen a single wild elephant since I arrived in Thailand," Sunday observed.

"You probably won't," Simon told her. "At one time, there were three hundred species of elephants."

"Three hundred *different* species?"

He nodded. "Now there are two—*Elephas maximus* and *Loxodanta africana.*"

"The Asian elephant and the African elephant."

"Less than a century ago two hundred thousand wild Asian elephants were said to roam the country of Thailand and its neighbors. Now, it's estimated that only a few thousand remain, most of them in captivity."

"What happened?"

"Ivory poachers. Thieves. Deforestation."

"That's tragic," Sunday said, feeling a genuine sense of loss.

They came to a fork in the road. Simon stopped, went down on his haunches and examined the trail. Then he straightened, raised his hand to shade the sunlight from his eyes and studied the surrounding mountains.

"We'll take the path on the right," he stated.

"By any chance, were you a Boy Scout?" Sunday inquired as she trotted alongside him.

He blinked. "As a matter of fact, I was."

She permitted herself a small sigh. "I'm not surprised."

"What makes you say that?"

"You seem right at home in the woods. And you
seem to know a lot about survival."

He made a sound of acknowledgment. "The navy."

Sunday shot a quick sideways glance at him. "What
about the navy?"

"That's where I learned survival."

"The city," she countered.

He scowled. "The city? What about the city?"

"That's where I learned survival."

Simon put his head back and laughed. Sunday realized that she loved the sound of his laughter. For
that matter, she loved the sound of his deep baritone
voice, whether he was talking, singing, whispering
sweet suggestions in her ear or groaning with pure un-
mitigated pleasure when they made love.

A woman should like—she should *love*—the sound
of a man's voice if she was going to spend the rest of
her life listening to it, Sunday admonished herself.

Was she going to spend the rest of her life with Simon?

The truth was, they'd never discussed the future.
They had only spoken occasionally of the past and
usually of the present, the here and now.

Could she imagine a future with Simon in it?

Could she imagine a future without him?

They hiked for another quarter of an hour, before
Simon announced, "We're almost there."

"Where is there?" she asked.

"The ancient elephant watering hole."

Sunday managed not to make a face. She could almost picture what an elephant watering hole must look like, its banks trampled and oozing with thick mud, its once crystal-clear waters turned dun brown, vultures perched in a nearby tree waiting patiently for the weak and sick animals to drop to the parched ground.

She couldn't have been more wrong. They came around a bend in the centuries-old track, and there, before them, was a pristine pond.

She reached for Simon's hand. "It's perfect."

"Yes, it is."

"Did you know it was here?"

He shook his head.

Terraced layers of rock had been fashioned by the forces of nature. A cascading waterfall dropped some fifty feet from the cliffs above into a series of descending pools. At the bottom was a placid pond, lush, green grass and verdant shade trees. There were songbirds in the branches overhead and small silvery fish in the water at their feet.

"It doesn't look like anyone, or anything, has been here in a long time," she observed.

"I would say it's been a *very* long time."

"The water is so clear, I can see the rocks on the bottom of the pond." Sunday wiped the perspiration from her upper lip with the back of her hand. She suddenly realized how hot and thirsty she was. "Do you think we could go swimming?"

Simon leaned over and dipped his hand in the water. "Nope."

"Why not?"

"The water is too cold."

She skimmed her fingers along the surface of the pond. "Brrrrr. It's ice-cold."

"Probably comes from the mountains," Simon said, dropping to the grass. "How about a drink of lukewarm water and a piece of fruit that Siri packed for us?"

"That's the best offer I've had all day," Sunday said, plunking herself down beside him.

It was some time later, after they'd shared several bananas and some cold rice, and taken turns sipping from Simon's canteen that Sunday leaned back on her elbows, raised her face to the noonday sun and murmured contentedly, "Now what?"

Simon shrugged. "I honestly don't know."

"Where do we go from here?"

"We don't go anywhere. This is it."

She opened her eyes and stared at him. "This is *what?*"

"The end of the trail. As far as we venture. Our final destination," he elaborated.

"There isn't a single Buddha in sight," she remarked, not in the least bit concerned by it.

"Not a one," Simon agreed.

Sunday couldn't quite stifle the yawn that overtook her.

"Tired?" he asked.

"Yes."

"We could take a few minutes of R and R, if you like," he suggested, stretching out lazily on the soft carpet of grass beside the tranquil pool.

"There aren't any nesting cobras around here, are there?" she inquired, half-serious.

"Nope."

"Are you certain?"

"I'm certain."

She couldn't resist teasing him just a little. "I wouldn't want to be bitten, you know."

"The only thing around here that's likely to bite you is me," Simon warned, pulling her down beside him.

Sunday went into his arms, and it was the most natural place in the world for her to be.

When had she so utterly and completely fallen in love with this man? After all, she'd known Simon for less than two weeks, a fortnight, some three hundred hours.

Was time an illusion when it came to matters of the heart?

Any further speculation came to an abrupt halt as Simon brought his mouth down on hers. He inhaled her breath, drank from her lips, filled his hands with her until Sunday knew that his embrace was truly heaven on earth.

"Heaven," she murmured.

Simon raised his head. "What?"

"Kissing you is heaven," she said, not really wanting to talk.

He went still.

She forced her eyes open, and looked at Simon. He had the oddest expression on his face. "What is it?"

He sat up, taking her with him. "You're brilliant."

She didn't understand. "Th-Thank you."

"You've given me an idea."

"It wouldn't be the first time," she said dryly.

"I didn't mean *that* kind of idea." Simon draped his arm across her shoulders. "Look around you, Sunday. What do you see?"

She realized he was serious. She looked around her. "I see a pond."

"Go on," he urged.

"I see trees and rocks and grass and blue skies."

"Keep going."

"The sun and a few white clouds."

"Lower," he suggested.

Sunday sank her teeth into her lip and vowed she was not going to glance down at Simon's lap. She cleared her throat. "There's a waterfall, of course."

"And?"

"Water."

"And?"

"Where the waterfall hits the rocks, there's a kind of mist..." Sunday allowed her voice to trail off.

"You might even say it was a—"

She saw what he was getting at. "Heavenly mist."

"Bingo!"

"The Hidden Buddha of the Heavenly Mist," she recited in its entirety. "Do you think it's possible?"

Simon gave a sigh. "I'm beginning to think anything is possible." He got to his feet and held his hand out to her. "C'mon, sweetheart, let's see if it's merely myth and legend, or if there's something to this map of yours."

They made their way around the pond in the direction of the waterfall. The closer they got, the clearer it became that there was something behind the curtain of water.

"Watch your step. The rocks are slippery," Simon indicated as they turned their backs to the stone cliffs and inched their way along a narrow ledge.

A fine mist covered both of them by the time they slipped behind the waterfall.

Then, for a moment, for an eternity, the only sound Sunday could hear was the thundering beat of her own heart. "Simon, look!" She pointed.

It was a door, man-made, oversize and expertly hewn from the natural stone. The entrance was encased in thick vines and jungle vegetation that had grown up over the centuries. In the center of the stone portal, covered with moss and ravaged by time, was a sculpture—a bas-relief—of an elephant.

"A sacred white elephant," Sunday murmured as she brushed away enough of the grime to reveal light-colored stone beneath.

Simon hacked away with his machete. They both put their weight and shoulders to the fulcrum point. Very slowly, the door began to open, and they stepped inside.

It was a large, vaulted, cavernous room. Natural sunlight flooded into the room from above. There was a great gaping hole in what had once been the ceiling, only a portion of which remained intact. The pile of rubble at their feet testified to where the remainder had gone.

"Whatever this place is," Sunday said, whispering, "it's definitely hidden."

"I think I know what it was," Simon spoke up.

"What?"

"A temple."

Trees—fig and silk-cotton trees, according to Simon—thrived on top of the temple walls. Their gnarled and twisting roots reached down like huge tentacles to grasp the tumbled-down stones. Sunday studied the intricate carvings on the stones: dancing figures, fierce dragons, great battles, demons and heavenly nymphs, and everywhere depictions of the sacred white elephant.

"An ancient temple?" she said in a hushed, reverent tone.

Simon rubbed his chin. "I'm no expert, of course, but I'd guess twelfth century."

Sunday found the thought mind-boggling. "That's almost a thousand years ago."

"Yup."

"Where do you think these stone steps lead?"

"Let's find out." Simon grasped her hand in his— he expertly balanced his machete in the other hand— and together they climbed the winding, narrow stairway.

It led to another, smaller room. The only object in the room was a pedestal. And there, sitting in the center of the pedestal, was a statue of the Buddha. It, too, was covered with snakelike vines and vegetation and a millenium of neglect.

The statue wasn't large and it wasn't small. From top to bottom, Sunday calculated, the seated figure was no more than four feet tall. It appeared to be carved from solid rock.

"White marble?" she speculated.

Simon nodded. "And no doubt weighs hundreds of pounds."

"That's odd," she said.

He came up to stand beside her. "What is?"

"The eyes are red. Isn't it unusual for the Buddha to be depicted with red eyes?"

"Very unusual."

Carefully, gingerly, Sunday pulled a vine away from the face of the statue. "There are bits of colored glass draped around the shoulders and the wrists, almost like a necklace and bracelet."

"It wasn't uncommon to adorn the Buddha. Some statues are encrusted with stones."

"Gemstones?"

"Precious and semiprecious gemstones, and sometimes just bits of colored glass," said Simon as he perused the temple chamber.

Sunday bent over and scooped up a handful of pebbles from the floor around the statue. The stones were all sizes and shapes, and ranged from pale pink to dark purple. Several of the larger ones were a deep, iridescent shade of red.

Sunday gazed at her palm. "Fire."

"What is?"

"The color of these rocks is like fire."

Simon peered over her shoulder. "Not fire. Blood."

Sunday wiped the stones against the pant leg of her jeans. What was it Simon had said to her on the journey from Chiang Mai? The answer came to her. The earlier settlers had built temples to Buddha and filled them with artifacts, religious treasures and rare pigeon's blood rubies.

Her hand began to shake. "Ohmigod!"

Stunned, she stood there for a moment without moving, without speaking.

Simon must have sensed her agitation. He slipped a supporting arm around her waist. "What is it, sweetheart?"

Sunday stared down at the stones. Could they be? Something told her they were.

"Rubies," she managed to say in a hoarse whisper.

Simon plucked one of the larger stones from her hand and examined it closely. "Could be," he allowed. "If they are, you're holding a fortune in your hand." He looked up at her with a thoughtful expression on his face. "The man who sold you the map did say it would lead you to happiness and riches."

She didn't want riches. Not this kind, anyway, Sunday realized. And she had already found all the happiness she could ever hope for in Simon's arms.

She took a deep breath and dropped the stones, one by one, into the lap of the Buddha. "They aren't mine," she stated unequivocally. "I came to Thailand in search of something. I believe I've found it."

"What about the rubies?"

"I don't want them," she said simply.

"Well, I do" came an icy cold voice from directly behind them as the ice-cold barrel of a gun was pressed into Sunday's back.

Thirteen

"**S**on of a bitch," Simon muttered under his breath.

"Turn around slowly," cautioned a masculine voice directly behind him.

There was something vaguely familiar about that voice, Simon realized, but he couldn't seem to put a face with it. Of course, identifying the bastard might well be the least of his problems. He had to buy himself some time—time to think, time to act, maybe time to save Sunday's neck and his. "What the—?"

"Mind your p's and q's, Hazard. My comrade has a gun pointed at Ms. Harrington's lovely back."

Simon started to turn around. "So help me God, if I ever get my hands on you!"

"Tut-tut. Speaking of hands, put yours behind your head where I'll be able to see them at all times."

Adrenaline was shooting into Simon's bloodstream. Every one of his senses was on red alert. But he understood the necessity of keeping his wits about him and maintaining a poker face. He knew only too well the price he and Sunday might pay if he didn't.

Hands behind his head, fingers interlaced, Simon slowly turned to face his adversary. "Nigel Grimwade," he stated, making certain that his expression and his tone gave nothing away. It was a technique he'd used to great advantage in big business.

Nigel's handsome features were momentarily marred by a boyish pout. "You don't seemed surprised, somehow, Hazard."

"I can't say that I am."

"What do you want me to do with the Harrington woman?" inquired Nigel's companion.

"Bring her over here," he said.

Simon gave a nod of acknowledgment. "Mrs. Grimwade."

The young woman laughed. "I'm not his wife."

The Grimwades' marital status—or the lack of it—was none of his concern. He was curious about one thing, however, Simon discovered. "What happened to your Australian accents?"

"We're not Australian," claimed the young woman.

"What are you, then?" asked Sunday as the two women joined the men.

"Classically trained," answered Nigel as he brandished his revolver at them.

"The Old Vic," added the female who had previously called herself his wife.

"Royal Shakespearean," Nigel chimed in.

Sunday made a disparaging sound. "You're actors!"

His reply was a sly one. "You might say that."

The woman was less reticent. "We're independent contractors. We serve anyone or any country that wants to hire us. And someone has hired us to follow the map."

Sunday tried a little acting of her own. "What map?"

"The map that idiotic man sold you in Bangkok when it had been promised to us," Millicent whined.

"Well, you know what they say, Millie," Simon offered. "Easy come, easy go."

"Maybe it's easy for you to say. You obviously don't care a whit about money and the things it can buy," she said, looking down her nose at his faded jeans and scuffed cowboy boots. "But some of us like the better things in life."

"The best things in life are free," Sunday piped up.

Their eyes met for an instant over the woman's head. Simon suddenly wished that he had some way of telling Sunday the things he could have said—should have said—last night and hadn't. Regrets: he found he had a few.

"Anyway, Nigel and I thought we had another lead in Chiang Mai, but when we met our contact at the marketplace, it turned out to be a red herring."

"It *was* the two of you I caught a glimpse of at the night market!" Sunday exclaimed.

"You saw us?"

"You saw them?" Simon took a step toward her, scowling. "You never mentioned that you saw the Grimwades—or whoever the hell they are—in Chiang Mai."

"I meant to, but it began to rain and we ran for shelter. I had other things on my mind." Sunday shrugged. "I forgot."

He was partially to blame, Simon knew. Those other things had been him.

He faced their opponents. "You lied. You didn't fly back to Bangkok."

"So we lied. So we didn't fly back to Bangkok," Millicent mocked. "So sue us."

"We've wasted enough time in idle chitchat," Nigel spoke up. "It's time to take care of business." He began to issue orders. "Millie, you keep your gun aimed at the Harrington woman, while I see to Mr. Hazard. I'm going to tie you securely to that pillar, Hazard," Nigel explained, producing a length of sturdy cord. "I know all about the fancy Beretta you keep in a holster down your back and the bowie knife in your cowboy boot, so no funny stuff."

"How the devil—?"

"I'm sorry, Simon," Sunday called out with a catch in her voice. "I said something to the others when those bandits stopped us that day on the road to Lamphun. I never dreamed it would be used against you."

"It's okay, sweetheart," he reassured her.

"So, that's the way the wind blows, does it? I thought as much," Nigel claimed as he yanked the rope around Simon's chest even tighter and secured the end in a knot.

"You're next," Millie said to Sunday, prodding her with the barrel of her revolver.

In less than five minutes, both he and Sunday were tied up and trussed like a pair of chickens.

"You won't be needing this any longer," Nigel informed him with a mirthless laugh as he removed the Beretta and tossed it away. "Nor this," he added, dispensing with the bowie knife.

"The rest of the job is going to be a piece of cake," the young man remarked to his female companion. "Gather up all the rubies you can, Millie. We'll sort out the most valuable stones later."

Laying their guns aside, they began to scoop up the priceless gems from the floor of the temple, the stone altar, even the lap of the Buddha, and dump them into the young woman's oversize handbag.

"We're going to be rich!" Millie squealed with delight.

"Yes, we are," Nigel agreed, holding up a particularly large stone to the sunlight. He let out a low whistle, quickly looked around and, when his partner in crime wasn't watching, slipped the huge unfaceted ruby into the pocket of his jacket.

Cripes, thought Simon with disgust, Nigel Grimwade wasn't even an honest thief!

"What are we going to do about those two?" the woman asked, glancing meaningfully over her shoulder at them.

"I haven't decided yet," Nigel told her. "Maybe we'll simply leave them here in this lovely old temple."

"They could die," Millie said.

"They could." Nigel shrugged and scooped up another handful of stones. "Or they could get lucky."

"I'm afraid *your* luck has just run out, old chap" came a clipped British voice.

Sunday's spirits soared. It was Arthur Bantry. Help was at hand. Good would now triumph over evil. They would be saved. All would be right with the world.

"Colonel Bantry, am I glad to see you!" she called out to him.

"Miss Harrington," he greeted her with just a hint of a reserved smile. "Mr. Hazard."

Arthur Egbert Bantry, dressed as always in an immaculate khaki uniform, was poised over the young couple who called themselves the Grimwades. He had Excalibur in his hand, the very sharp point of which was pressed against Nigel's jugular.

"No. Don't bother getting up, young man," he said in a deceptively mild tone. "I think I prefer you and the young lady on your hands and knees."

Millicent raised her head and attempted to bat her eyelashes at the gentleman. "This isn't what you think, Colonel," she said in a baby-doll voice.

He laughed; it was a surprisingly chilling sound. "Don't waste your breath, Miss...whatever your name is. I was in the business long before you were even born. It will take a great deal more than a third-rate—and I am giving you, and your so-called part-ner, the benefit of the doubt—pair of actors to get the best of me." The Colonel kicked a length of cord in her direction. "Tie up Nigel nice and tight."

Millie started to get to her feet. "But—"

Arthur Bantry quickly armed himself with one of the guns they had laid down in their haste to gather up the rubies. He pointed the weapon at Millicent's heart. "You might like to keep several things in mind—I am an expert marksman, and Nigel here slipped a bauble into his pocket while you weren't looking. If it's a first-rate stone, and I dare say it is, it could be worth several million pounds."

The young woman shot sharp daggers at her part-ner. "Nigel, you cheat, you scum, you—"

Nigel Grimwade winced as the rope dug into his flesh. "I was going to share it with you, Millie. Hon-est."

"There is no honor among thieves," admonished Colonel Bantry. "You should remember that, young lady."

Once Nigel was restrained, Arthur Bantry quickly saw to the young woman, as well. Only then, Sunday noticed, was Excalibur returned to the Colonel's walking stick.

"Does anyone mind if I smoke?" the gentleman politely inquired as if the five of them were in attendance at a garden party or having cocktails together. He took a cigarette case and a holder from an inside jacket pocket, and withdrew an unfiltered cigarette.

"So that's why your hands were always shaking, why you were always fingering your moustache," Sunday said. "You're a smoker, but you weren't smoking."

"Bad for the image."

"The image?"

"In this business, everyone is an actor," he said expansively. "Smoking didn't fit the part I was playing this time."

"Next, you'll be telling us 'all the world's a stage,'" she said, trying to hold her chin high. For, somewhere in the middle of her conversation with Arthur Bantry, Sunday had realized that he had no intentions of setting them free. She and Simon might well never leave this ancient temple.

She wished she'd told Simon last night what had been in her heart and on the tip of her tongue. Now she might never have the chance to tell him. She had to buy them time, time to think, time to plan, time to act, to say what needed to be said.

She looked up at the British gentleman. "I'm deeply disappointed in you, Colonel."

"I know you are, Miss Harrington."

"You're nothing but a petty thief."

He glanced down at Millicent's handbag. "I wasn't after the map, you know. Although I believe I will keep the rubies, as long as you've found them."

"But if you weren't after the promised riches..."
Then why had he followed them?

Arthur Bantry permitted himself a small sigh. "I do have my share of regrets, Miss Harrington. Perhaps if we had met at another time, another place—" khaki shoulders were raised and then lowered again "—or if you hadn't been with Hazard."

She was puzzled. "What does Simon have to do with it?"

His forehead crinkled into a genuine frown. "Everything."

"I don't understand."

"I believe Hazard does."

When Simon spoke, Sunday could hear the underlying anger and absolute determination in his voice. "So, *you* were the one who left Jonathan to die."

Sunday sucked in her breath.

Arthur Bantry put a cigarette in the ivory holder, raised it to his lips, held a match to the tip and took a long draw on the end before he answered. "I see you finally put two and two together."

"Finally."

"Jonathan Hazard was a professional, just as I was. We professionals understand these things. It was a regrettable piece of business."

"Regrettable?" Simon repeated.

"The outcome."

"He was supposed to die."

The Colonel nodded his head and continued to puff away. "He was supposed to quietly disappear without a trace."

Simon stiffened beside her. "You bastard," he swore harshly under his breath.

Cold eyes narrowed to two thin slits behind a column of cigarette smoke. "It's all water under the bridge now, if you'll pardon the pun. Jonathan Hazard has left the business, and so have I."

Sunday had an odd feeling in the pit of her stomach. "But you still intend to take the rubies and vamoose, leaving the four of us here to die."

"As Nigel said, you could get lucky." Arthur Bantry studied the crumbling temple. "Actually, you youngsters may have done me a real service," he said, addressing the pair of former thespians. "Should anyone ever stumble upon this place, it will be *your* fingerprints, *your* guns, *your* ropes, *your* bones—" a feral grin spread across his face from ear to ear "—that are left as clues. It will make for a beautifully staged scene."

Sunday's heart was galloping. "Scene?"

The stub of the Colonel's cigarette was pinched flat between his thumb and finger, then deposited in his pants pocket. "Wouldn't want to leave any evidence behind, now, would I?"

Sunday was willing to reason with him, even plead with him. "But, Colonel..."

"I am sorry, Miss Harrington. But I win, and you lose."

A strong, confident female voice spoke from the stone steps behind him. "I'm afraid *I* win, and *you* lose, Colonel."

Five heads snapped around.

"My God, it's the nun!" exclaimed Nigel Grimwade.

"And she's got a gun," added Millicent unnecessarily.

"Good grief," muttered Simon.

"Sister Agatha Anne," said Sunday.

"'Hail, hail, the gang's all here,'" Simon growled near her ear.

"The more the merrier," she whispered back, tempering a nervous urge to laugh.

The young nun looked the same—except for the gun in her right hand, of course—but she was far from sounding like the sweet, shy, demure and retiring Sister Agatha Anne they had all known on the journey north.

"No one speaks unless I give them permission." Her voice snapped with authority. However, the lethal weapon she was pointing straight at the Colonel spoke louder than any words.

"Do you have any idea who you're dealing with?" Arthur Bantry demanded with just the right touch of righteous indignation.

"I know exactly *who* and *what* you are, Colonel," the nun replied, cool as a cucumber.

Apparently, he wasn't ready to give up. "And just who do you think you are, young lady?"

"It won't do you any good to bluster on so, Bantry," said the slight figure in the nun's habit. "I'm with M16."

The effect of that statement on Arthur Bantry was quite astounding, Sunday witnessed. She turned her head and whispered to Simon, "What is M16?"

"Britain's secret service," he whispered back.

"Really?"

"It was once the world's premier intelligence service. Now it's mainly known because of the James Bond movies."

"You mean 007, licensed to kill?"

"Yup."

Sunday completely forgot about lowering her voice to a whisper. "Sister Agatha Anne is a spy!"

"Not exactly," responded the woman with the gun.

Sunday blinked several times in quick succession. "You're not a spy?"

"I'm not a nun."

"I knew it!" Sunday informed them all. "That first day, before we even left Bangkok, I thought to myself—none of these people are what or who they claim to be."

"You should have trusted your instincts," said Sister Agatha Anne.

She arched a questioning eyebrow at the young woman still dressed in the habit of a nun. "Mother Superior isn't a spy, too, is she?"

The woman smiled. "Mother Superior is exactly what she appears to be." Her attention reverted to Arthur Bantry. "You should have stayed retired, Arthur. We've known for the past several years that you were working both sides, of course, that you were taking money from anyone and everyone who was willing to pay you."

He sniffed. "A man has to live."

"I understand you live very well. First-class all the way."

"And why not? I deserve to. All those years slaving for queen and country. Nobody gave a damn."

"Perhaps not," Agatha Anne said quietly. "But you gave your sworn oath and you have broken that oath."

Arthur Bantry's shoulders slumped forward like those of a defeated man.

Apparently, the agent posing as Sister Agatha Anne was not so easily fooled into believing his sudden submission, however. "Carefully let your walking stick drop to the floor, Colonel."

He did as she ordered.

"We're the innocent parties in this whole affair," whined Nigel Grimwade. "Millie and I were just a couple of tourists who got mixed up in something we didn't understand."

"You can cut the balderdash," said the nun with the gun. "I know who you and Millie are, too."

"Well, aren't you the bloody genius!" Nigel swore, turning ugly.

Sunday got an elbow in her back. It was Simon's.

"Cover for me," he whispered urgently.

"Cover for you?"

"I have to reach my left boot."

"Why?"

"There is an old saying—"

Her eyes looked heavenward. "Of course. There always is."

"'Beware the weapon a man does not show you.'"

Sunday talked out of the side of her mouth. "You have another weapon on you?"

He nodded. "A second knife. I need to get it and cut us free. My gut feeling is this business is going to get nastier and nastier."

"I agree."

"On the count of three, fall over sideways like you've just fainted," he instructed.

"I'll do my best." But she was no actress, Sunday wanted to point out to him.

"One. Two. Three."

Sunday pretended to swoon. She made a low, moaning sound, dropped her head to her chest and slumped to one side.

Simon moved in the opposite direction.

"I believe this has been too much for Miss Harrington," observed the Colonel. "Perhaps I should offer her some assistance."

"Stay where you are, Bantry," ordered the nun.

It all happened very quickly. The Colonel turned and nimbly threw himself at Sister Agatha Anne's ankles. The long skirt of her habit was a distinct disadvantage, of course. She teetered this way and that way, and finally toppled to the floor of the temple.

The revolver in her hand went flying through the air, and as luck would have it, landed at Simon's feet. The rope that had held them like trussed chickens snapped like a rubber band. Simon had obviously recovered the knife from his other boot.

Sword poised to strike—the Colonel appeared perfectly willing to use his blade on Sister Agatha Anne—Simon grabbed the man's arm, twisted it behind his back and disarmed him.

Then, with Excalibur in one hand and the British agent's revolver in the other, Simon stood and glared at them for a moment. Then he issued his edict. "Listen up, people. From now on, we do this my way." He looked at each of them in turn. "We'll make this nice and simple. Which one of you *isn't* a spy?"

Fourteen

"You aren't a spy, are you?" Sunday inquired as they made their way from the Mae Hong Son police station to the local Holiday Inn later that night.

"Nope."

She took in a deep breath and let it out again. "I'm so relieved. I was beginning to wonder if anyone in this crazy business was who or what they claimed to be."

Simon had been wonderful through the whole ordeal: taking charge of the situation, clearing up any misunderstandings, translating for those who didn't speak the language. It was only now that they were alone that he had become strangely pensive, she realized as they strolled along Mae Hong Son's one main street.

Sunday attempted to lighten his mood. "When we started this journey to the City of Mist, I certainly didn't expect the jail to be the first thing I saw when we finally got to town."

"Me, neither."

"I'm not sorry about the Grimwades, but I confess I'm disappointed in the Colonel."

"He had me fooled, too."

"When did you realize he was the double agent who had tried to kill Jonathan?" she asked, as if it were a perfectly normal thing to be asking someone.

"Only once we were all in the temple." Simon stuffed his hands deep into the pockets of his jeans. "I told you, Sunday. I was a businessman back in the States. I don't know anything about being a secret agent or a spy."

"The Colonel assumed you were a threat."

"Apparently."

"He saw you as some kind of avenging angel."

"'Vengeance is mine, I will repay, saith the Lord,'" Simon quoted.

"In the end, it was you who saved the day," she noted.

"It was stupid, Sunday," Simon stated, berating himself. "I could easily have gotten us both killed. These people are playing for keeps, and I pretended it was all a glorious adventure, part of the services provided by your hired tour guide."

"You're being awfully hard on yourself." She reached out and patted his arm. "After all, as you said, you aren't a secret agent or a spy."

They walked for a time without speaking. Sunday looked up at the stars overhead and the moon on the rise. There were some kind of flowers in bloom along the street; their scent was sweet and poignant. "What will happen to the others now?" she asked.

"The Colonel and the Grimwades will be sent back to England to stand trial. Unless they strike a bargain. The British government doesn't like to be embarrassed. They may decide it's better to keep the scandal out of the newspapers."

"I noticed that Sister Agatha Anne never bothered to explain herself to the local authorities. She kept on her habit and the distinctive headpiece the whole while we were at the police station. It wouldn't surprise me if the people here still believe she's a nun," Sunday said.

"It wouldn't surprise me, either."

"It does explain Mother Superior's attitude concerning Sister Agatha Anne that first day in Bangkok."

"Yes, it does." He looked at her askance. "Are you sure you don't mind about the rubies? They would have looked stunning on you with your red hair."

Sunday shook her head and kicked at a pebble in the street. "The rubies belong exactly where they are—with the Thai authorities. With any luck, some of the money will be used to help the hill-tribe people."

"With any luck."

"I suppose the archaeologists will have a field day with the Hidden Buddha of the Heavenly Mist."

"I suppose they will."

"The waterfall, the pristine pond, the green grass, the ancient Buddhist temple—none of it will ever be the same, will it?"

"Nope."

"It will never be just ours again."

"I'm afraid not."

She was trembling with emotion. "What was it you told me about change?"

There was a sardonic tone to Simon's voice. "I said change was inevitable."

"Yes, you did." She kicked at another stone. "And you were right. It is inevitable."

"That doesn't mean we always have to like it," he told her.

They reached the Holiday Inn, and Simon escorted her to the door of her room. Sunday put the key in the lock and turned. The door opened. She turned to face him. There was an awkward silence between them.

"It's been quite a day. You must be exhausted," he said.

"It has been and I am."

He concentrated on his hands. "Besides, there's always tomorrow."

Sunday glanced down at the watch on her wrist. "It is tomorrow."

He looked up and frowned. "What?"

"It's after midnight. It is tomorrow."

"You'd better get some sleep. The return trip to Bangkok is a long one."

"Good night, Simon," she called out softly, but he had already closed the door to his room.

Sunday shut and locked her door. She turned with a sigh and looked over the hotel room. There was a bed, a dresser, a closet and what she hoped and prayed was a bathroom with modern plumbing.

Upon closer examination, she found the bathroom was small, compact and clean. It also had a second door. A door that appeared to connect with the room next door.

Simon's room was next door.

Sunday took hold of the doorknob and turned. It was unlocked.

She knocked. Once. Twice. Three times. Softly, but loud enough to be heard.

"Come in!" a familiar voice called out.

Sunday opened the second bathroom door and walked directly into Simon's hotel room. It was identical to her own.

"This is your room," she said.

"Yes."

"We share a bathroom."

"I know."

"Our rooms are essentially connecting rooms."

"Essentially."

Sunday planted her hands on her hips. "A fact that you failed to mention to me."

"I didn't know until thirty seconds ago."

"Oh."

"As long as you're here, do you have everything you need?" Simon inquired as if he were back in the guise of tour guide.

Sunday burst out with it. "No, I don't."

He ran his eyes over her. "What don't you have that you need?"

Sunday raised her eyes and looked intently into his. She opened her heart and mind. She put fear and cowardice and self-consciousness behind her. If she wanted a future, she was going to have to take a chance. She steeled herself. "No guts, no glory."

"What?"

"No guts, no glory. Nothing ventured, nothing gained. Life is an adventure. Grab it with both hands. Go for the gusto."

"I've heard it all before."

"I know. You said it all to me."

"What are you getting at, Sunday?"

She wouldn't start from the beginning. She'd start somewhere in the middle. "I came to Thailand looking for something."

"So did I."

"I found it."

"I did, too."

This was important. "What was it?" she asked.

Simon combed his fingers through his hair. It was still long, still curly, still uncut, she noted. He gave her his answer. "What I found was an appreciation for being alive."

"I have never met a man who was more alive than you, Simon Hazard."

"What did you find, Sunday Harrington? Inspiration for your designer label? The silk material you've been wanting to work with? The kind of crafts you were searching for? The people to make them?"

Sunday bit the inside of her mouth. "I found all of those things, of course."

He wagged his finger at her. "But? I can hear the *but* in your voice, sweetheart."

She took a deliberate step toward him. "But I found something far more important than all of that."

Simon didn't move a muscle. He seemed glued to the spot. "You did?"

She took another step. "I did."

They were toe-to-toe, leg-to-leg, hip-to-hip, chest-to-breast, chin-to-chin, eye-to-eye.

Simon apparently had to know. "What was it you found?"

"You," she said with simplicity.

He exhaled.

Sunday reached up and dropped a kiss on the hard line of his jaw. "It doesn't matter *what* you were before, or *who* you were before, Simon, I want to spend the rest of my life with you. I think you can become my best friend, my lover, my husband and the father of my children."

"Why?"

"Because I love you."

Sunday loved him.

He wanted to shout it from the rooftops, the mountaintops, from the top of the tallest building. Unfortunately, the tallest building in Mae Hong Son was the two-story Holiday Inn where they were staying.

"You love me." He tried it on for size. It fit perfectly.

Sunday said it again. "I love you."

Simon picked her up and swung her around the room. "You love me. You love me. You love me." He savored the moment, the feeling, but he knew what came next. And there were one or two things he had to get off his chest first.

He put Sunday down on her feet. He began to pace back and forth in front of her. He finally paused and suggested, "You might like to sit down," he said, indicating the only chair in the room.

She sat down.

"There are a few things about me you don't know," he said in preamble.

"That's to be expected. We met less than two weeks ago," she said reasonably.

He was shocked. "Has it been less than two weeks?"

"Twelve days, to be precise."

"But who's counting?" they said in unison.

Simon took the plunge. "I didn't actually lie to you, Sunday. It was more a sin of omission."

Her face fell. "You're married."

"Yes. No. Only to you."

She brightened. "Then nothing else matters."

He didn't agree. "I don't want to start our married life with anything between us."

Her face fell again. "You have children."

"I can guarantee that I don't have any children."

Her face lit up. "Would you like to?"

"Well, of course, I would like to have children one day, but we digress." Sometimes the woman was infuriating, maddening, sometimes she drove him crazy.

"It can't be that bad," she advised.

"It's not. It is. It depends on your point of view."

"Well?"

"I'm not really a tour guide."

She started to get up.

"Wait, there's more."

She sat down again.

Simon was frantically pacing back and forth now. "I don't know any other way of saying it." He stopped, turned and faced her. "I'm a wealthy man, sweetheart. I have my own business. Actually, I have my own businesses. I have an island. I have a penthouse. Hell, I was a bloody millionaire before I was thirty."

Sunday stood up, wrapped her arms around his waist and whispered in his ear, "So was I, darling."

"You were?"

"Actually, I was a bloody millionaire before I was twenty-five—"

"But who's counting?" they said together.

Simon took this most precious woman into his arms and gazed down into her eyes. "Have I told you that I love you?"

"No."

"I love you."

"There will be so much to see to," Sunday began to fret some time later. It was nearly dawn and they had been making love all night long. "We don't even know what city we'll live in . . . what state . . . what country."

"Darling," Simon murmured as he dropped a kiss on her bare shoulder and began to settle himself between her thighs, "a wise man once said something."

"What?"

"*Where* you are isn't as important as *who* you're with."

"What wise man?" she whispered as he came to her.

"This wise man, this very, very lucky man. . . ."

Epilogue

Sunday Harrington and Simon Hazard were married many times: by Tget, the headman of the hill tribe in the north of Thailand, of course, then in a special ceremony at the Buddhist monastery where Simon had lived with the saffron-robed monks, and finally, with the blessings of Mother Superior, in the chapel at St. Agnes's.

Upon returning to the United States several months later, Sunday and Simon were joined in holy matrimony one last time in front of their families and friends. It was a joyous occasion.

The Siam collection was a resounding success. With the blessing of the newlyweds, the profits were used to create jobs for the hill-tribe craftspeople of northern

Thailand, and to establish a sanctuary for the last of the wild Asian elephants.

And when the time came to select a name for his wife's exclusive line of baby clothes and accessories for the nursery, Simon Hazard was the first to suggest *Sunday's Child*.

* * * * *

A Word About Rubies

The finest rubies come from Myanmar (Burma) and are more valuable per carat than emeralds, diamonds or sapphires. The enormous Timur ruby, a 352-carat stone known as the "Tribute to the World" was presented to Queen Victoria in 1851. It is carved with Arabic inscriptions giving dates and owners, and is part of the Royal jewels.

Rubies are said to protect their owner from harm and adverse fortune, to preserve physical and mental health and to control amorous desires.

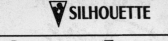

SILHOUETTE

Desire

COMING NEXT MONTH

MYSTERIOUS MOUNTAIN MAN
Annette Broadrick

Man of the Month

Rebecca Adams needed Jake Taggart. Only he could save her company. But he was living halfway up a mountain and she was going to have to go and get him. They'd be alone in the wilderness…

IMPULSE
Lass Small

Amy Allen took one look at Chas Cougar and decided she just had to meet him, so she decided to pose as a distant cousin and gate-crash the wedding he was attending. Chas knew right away Amy wasn't kin, but he could change that…if she was willing to be wed!

THE COP AND THE CHORUS GIRL
Nancy Martin

Opposites Attract

A cop couldn't ignore a female in distress, but it was unusual for a bride to rush away from the church before the wedding, which was why Patrick Flynn didn't react as quickly as Dixie wanted. Now he was going to have to fight off her gangster groom.

SILHOUETTE

Desire

COMING NEXT MONTH

DREAM WEDDING
Pamela Macaluso

Just Married

Once Alex would have sold his soul to kiss Genie. Now his "dream girl" was a prim teacher and the swot she'd rejected, who'd turned into a strapping, sexy CEO, was back for revenge.

HEAVEN CAN'T WAIT
Linda Turner

Spellbound

Prudence Sullivan knew Zeb Murdock was the lover for whom she'd waited centuries. Unfortunately, although he felt the fire between them, Murdock was determined to resist her. Pru couldn't allow that!

FORSAKEN FATHER
Kelly Jamison

Rachel Tucker had to resist rekindling the past—or risk revealing the secret she should have told John McClennon years ago. She had to protect her son.

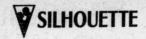

SILHOUETTE

> SPECIAL EDITION <

COMING NEXT MONTH

A MAN FOR MUM Gina Ferris Wilkins

That Special Woman! and the first book in her exciting new mini-series, *The Family Way*.

Seth Fletcher could see why mother-of-two Rachel Evans took life so seriously, but he was just the man to see that she had a regular dose of love and laughter!

A SECRET AND A BRIDAL PLEDGE Andrea Edwards

This Time, Forever

Although in the witness-protection programme, Amy Warren fought to keep her independence—a battle that pitted her against U.S. Marshal Mark Miller, who was trying to protect her. But why did he seem so familiar?

DOES ANYONE KNOW WHO ALLISON IS? Tracy Sinclair

Searching for her true identity Allison Riley might have found true love—and true heartbreak. Gabriel Rockford had been hired to uncover Allison's secrets, but he was having trouble keeping an open mind...

TRULY MARRIED Phyllis Halldorson

When his ex-wife was accused of murder, Fergus Lachlan had to dash to the rescue. No one else would ever have the motivation he did to prove Sharon innocent; no one else wanted to spend the rest of their life with her!

A STRANGER IN THE FAMILY Patricia McLinn

Bodie Smith had just discovered he had a sixteen-year-old son. So he went to the Weston Ranch and soon realized that his son wasn't the only person he could love who lived there.

A PERFECT SURPRISE Caroline Peak

Delivering a rain-soaked Labrador back to its owner was a good deed for Maggie Sullivan that really paid off. She got to meet his marvellous sexy, single, *male* owner.

♥ SILHOUETTE

Sensation

COMING NEXT MONTH

RESTLESS WIND Nikki Benjamin

Taylor Brannigan hadn't listened to the warning that she was a
target for a ruthless criminal. Now kidnapped and alone with the
enigmatic, magnetic Ross MacGregor, it looked as if that mistake
might be her last. Just as disturbing, Taylor couldn't understand the
strange longing she felt for her abductor…

POINT OF NO RETURN Rachel Lee

Under Blue Wyoming Skies

Sheriff Nathan Tate was hunting desperate criminals, but he was
also facing trouble at home. A tall, dark, handsome *younger* man
was threatening the love he'd thought could withstand anything.
Could his wife have betrayed him?

NIGHTSHADE Nora Roberts

He Who Dares & Night Tales

Colt Nightshade was looking for a friend's young daughter and he
needed local police help, Althea Grayson's help (some of you may
remember Althea from *Night Shift*). Althea was all business, even
though Colt was being distracted by thoughts of mutual pleasure.
How was he to woo this serious lady?

STILL MARRIED Diana Whitney

Suddenly, here was Kelsey, only a signature away from being his
ex-wife, back in Luke Sontag's life again. Asking him to help her.
Forcing him to face the passion and heartache that was their past.
What of the future?

SILHOUETTE

Intrigue

COMING NEXT MONTH

RISKY BUSINESS M.J. Rodgers

She was running for her life. He was trying to forget the past. Dana Carmody and Gil Webb met on a rain-drenched night, high on a cliff overlooking San Francisco bay. Two strangers who embraced in a kiss—that saved both of their lives.

PRIVATE EYES Madeline St. Claire

Private investigator Bill Donelan wanted to protect Lauren Pierce who was playing girl-friend to one of their clients. But because he wanted to possess her himself, seeing her engaged in hanky-panky with another man was hard to take…

GUILTY AS SIN Cathy Gillen Thacker

In defending charismatic Jake Lockhart, attorney Susan Kilpatrick could make her name—if she won a not-guilty verdict. But all the evidence pointed to his being a lady-killer who had committed a crime of passion. Would she succumb to Jake's charms and become his next female victim?

UNDER THE KNIFE Tess Gerritsen

Dr. Kate Chesne knew that no surgery was ever routine, but when a colleague and friend perished during a simple operation, her professional expertise was questioned. No one, and especially not the prosecuting attorney David Ransom, believed in her innocence. Would she be found guilty of malpractice…or murder?

A years supply of Silhouette Desires — absolutely free!

Would you like to win a years supply of seductive and breathtaking romances? Well, you can and they're FREE! All you have to do is complete the wordsearch puzzle below and send it to us by 31st March 1996. The first 5 correct entries picked after that date will win a years supply of Silhouette Desire novels (six books every month — worth over £150). What could be easier?

STOCKHOLM	PARIS	HELSINKI	ANKARA
REYKJAVIK	LONDON	ROME	AMSTERDAM
COPENHAGEN	PRAGUE	VIENNA	OSLO
MADRID	ATHENS	LIMA	

N	O	L	S	O	P	A	R	I	S
E	Q	U	V	A	F	R	O	K	T
G	C	L	I	M	A	A	M	N	O
A	T	H	E	N	S	K	E	I	C
H	L	O	N	D	O	N	H	S	K
N	S	H	N	R	I	A	O	L	H
E	D	M	A	D	R	I	D	E	O
P	R	A	G	U	E	U	Y	H	L
O	A	M	S	T	E	R	D	A	M
C	R	E	Y	K	J	A	V	I	K

Please turn over for details on how to enter ➡

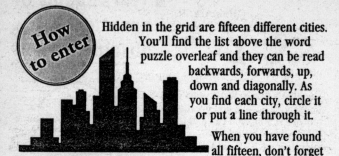

How to enter

Hidden in the grid are fifteen different cities. You'll find the list above the word puzzle overleaf and they can be read backwards, forwards, up, down and diagonally. As you find each city, circle it or put a line through it.

When you have found all fifteen, don't forget to fill in your name and address in the space provided below and pop this page in an envelope (you don't need a stamp) and post it today. Hurry – competition ends 31st March 1996.

Silhouette Capital Wordsearch
FREEPOST
Croydon
Surrey
CR9 3WZ

Are you a Reader Service Subscriber?   Yes ❑   No ❑

Ms/Mrs/Miss/Mr _____

Address _____

_____

_____ Postcode _____

One application per household.

You may be mailed with other offers from other reputable companies as a result of this application. If you would prefer not to receive such offers, please tick box.   ❑

COMP295
C

mps MAILING PREFERENCE SERVICE